FLORIDA,

A Love Story

CECILY CROSSMAN

Florida, A Love Story

Editor:
Trish Harris

Proofreaders:
Christie Alexander
Cyndie Cox
Connie McDonald

Cover and Interior Layout & Design:
Tarsha L. Campbell

Published by:
DOMINIONHOUSE
Publishing & Design, LLC
P.O. Box 681938 | Orlando, Florida 32868
www.mydominionhouse.com
407.703.4800 phone

DEDICATION
• • •

To all of you who love Florida,

    - from the panhandle which we lovingly call the Redneck Riviera, to Key West, where we can enter an Ernest Hemingway look-alike contest or celebrate Fantasy Fest where anything goes

    - for those who love our flora and fauna, our swamp lands and woods, our indigenous wildlife, and work to keep them flourishing

    - for those who love our warm winters, including our visitors from all over the world who make our lives richer in various ways

    - for those who love our hot summers, especially those of us who love to swim in our beautiful pools and enjoy our 825 miles of breathtakingly beautiful beaches

    - for my family and friends who are there for me, winter and summer, in good times and bad,

I dedicate this book, Florida, A Love Story

• • •

Old Florida Facts:

*"Florida, sir, is not worth buying. It is
a land of swamps, of quagmires, of frogs
and alligators and mosquitoes! A man, sir
would not immigrate into Florida. No, sir!
No man would immigrate into Florida no,
not from hell itself."*

- U. S. Rep. John Randolph of Virginia during debate on

giving Florida statehood in 1845.

ACKNOWLEDGEMENTS
• • •

*T*hank you:

To my enormously talented editor, Trish Harris, for taking my unwieldy manuscript and wrestling it to the ground until it finally emerged into the beautiful, historical novel I had envisioned. And, despite all of this, we are even closer friends than we have been for the past 25 years.

To Tarsha Campbell, DOMINIONHOUSE publisher, art and graphic designer and so much more, for overseeing every step of the publishing process.

To Christie Alexander, my dear friend and meticulous, highly skilled, primary proofreader, along with her other innumerable gifts and talents.

To John Crossman for encouraging me, in words and deeds, almost daily for the past several years, to share my words.

To Scott Crossman for providing the map of Florida in 1839 on the book cover. This was six years prior to Florida becoming a state and 32 years prior to the Civil War.

To each person who has generously written an endorsement for *Florida, A Love Story.*

Old Florida Facts:

Florida's old-time cowboys used whips made of braided leather. Snapping these whips made a loud "crack." That sound earned the cowboys the nickname "crackers."

ENDORSEMENTS

• • •

From the precise methods used to prepare and serve food and drinks; to the experiences of individuals from different races, cultures and backgrounds living in "harmony;" to the importance of lining hymns and other traditions of the early church; Cecily Crossman takes the reader on a delightful journey back in time in *Florida, A Love Story*. The novel moves at a rapid pace, delving long enough in the different settings to steep the reader in the moment. Avid bookworms and casual readers, alike, will appreciate the opportunity to escape to Florida past, and witness a respectable love story.

-Mildred Graham
Director-Advancement and Alumni Affairs
Florida A&M University College of Law
Advancement and Alumni Affairs

This is a touching historical fiction love story set in Central Florida in the late 1800s. I enjoyed learning about Florida history through the main characters and their many stories.

-Debra Schwinn
President, Palm Beach Atlantic University

As a fourth generation Floridian who has never lived outside of the state of Florida, I have never learned so much about the only place I have called home. The craftsmanship that combined the history and fiction allowed me to explore our history while maintaining my interest in the lives of the characters. I finished the book with a deep appreciation for the cultures that have contributed to the state of Florida. I hope that readers take a sense of pride in the rich history of Florida after reading this piece of art.

-Charee Williams

I have been a docent at the Orange County Regional History Center for over 10 years. Ms. Crossman in her book *Florida, A Love Story* has taken Florida history and made it into a very interesting, very accurate, and understandable storybook about both history and life. It keeps the reader in suspense and makes one want to continue to the end without putting it down!!! Well done Cecily.

-Lou Williams
Ten Year Docent, Orange County Regional History Center

Cecily Crossman has written an intriguing story of love, revenge, and courage set within the backdrop of Central Florida in the 1880s. As a third generation Orlandoan, I learned a great deal about this region by following the exploits of the main characters as they traveled the area. I was fascinated, for example, by the description of a seemingly simple trip to the beach. *Florida, A Love Story* is a compelling tale, rich in area history, with an ending not to be missed.

-Rex V. McPherson II
R.D. Keene Trust

I love historical novels. This is a page turner for sure. Set in Central Florida and around all the little towns we go through today makes the story so relatable.

-Beth Payan

● ● ●

Old Florida Facts:

In 1840, five years before Florida became a state, there was not a single permanent pioneer living in what is now Orange, Seminole and Osceola counties.

TABLE OF CONTENTS

TABLE OF CONTENTS

TABLE OF CONTENTS

TABLE OF CONTENTS

TABLE OF CONTENTS

•••

Old Florida Facts:

Florida, which joined the union as the 27th state in 1845, is nicknamed the Sunshine State due to its unusual number of sunny days.

Preface
• • •

Florida, A Love Story

In 2000, the beginning of the new millennium, I began a quest to learn everything I could about historic Florida, and, more specifically, Central Florida, where I've lived for much of my adult life.

I read all the Florida history I could find. I interviewed folks who were third or fourth generation Floridians. They were not easy to find because, even today, most Floridians are from someplace else.

I revisited the heartbreaking history of the Civil War.

Somewhere along the line I started writing what would turn out to be, decades later, this book. It is a love letter to Florida, one of the last states to be civilized, where cattle roamed free and only the strong survived the miserable summers prior to air conditioning.

Our story begins in the year 1884, with Coleman Wills roaming through Central Florida, on horseback, as he'd done for most of his life. But this day he comes upon Catherine Hamilton, a northerner, trying unsuccessfully to bury her husband who had been murdered that morning.

Together they travel across Central Florida, with Cole helping Catherine seek revenge. Along the way, they encounter multiple adventures.

Although the story is a work of fiction, the setting and the highlighted sections about Florida, found throughout the book, are historically correct.

-Cecily Crossman

Old Florida Facts:

Orange County Florida's first settlers had to be almost self-sufficient because they were so few and far between. They raised their own food, built their own houses and furniture, and made their own clothes.

• • •

"When Cole came closer to the ranch, he could see what was left of an outbuilding, smoldering in the distance. The house, barn, and other buildings appeared to be untouched by the blaze."

CHAPTER ONE

Dirt to Dirt

• • •

The year was 1884 and it was Coleman Wills' 32nd birthday. He was spending it as he had every birthday for the past 15 years—riding alone across the Florida countryside. As Cole rode over the low slope, banked by giant live oaks and tall, long-leaf pines, he saw smoke in the distance. He knew it was coming from the Hamilton Ranch. Just two days before, when he had been buying supplies at the general store in Sanford, even the fern growers standing around outside had been discussing the "damn Yankee" and his wife who had come to Central Florida to raise cattle. "It's like the dang king and queen of England decided to take up ranchin' in the middle of the swamp! They don't know nothin' about nothin."

Cole Wills was a cowboy, a negative term in Florida. Years later cowboys would be romanticized as strong, trustworthy, self-reliant, brave American heroes who drove cattle across lonely, dangerous fields and swamplands. But at this time, most folks knew that cowboys didn't own anything, including stock, and considered them to be irresponsible drifters. When Cole wasn't serving as a preacher or lawman or healer of all sorts of physical ailments, he was a cowboy. He owned nothing, except what he carried with him.

The week before, he had come back from Kissimmee in south Orange County where he helped drive a herd of 20,000 cattle to Tampa and stayed long enough to see them loaded onto boats headed for Cuba. Cole had lived in Orange County all his life.

Covering all of Central Florida, the county stretched from Kissimmee to the south, and north, all the way to Sanford, where it bordered Lake Monroe. The lake was the widest part of the St. Johns River, which originated 50 miles east at the Atlantic Ocean. Orange County was the largest cattle-raising area in the United States, including Texas. And during the last quarter of the nineteenth century, cattle raising continued to grow in importance. But life was changing. Railroad barons like Henry Plant and Henry Flagler were slowly planting tracks through Central Florida, but the railroad empire builders were no match for the cattlemen. Florida, a cattle baron's magnet with its open ranges, would be one of the last cattle states to adopt fencing laws.

When Cole came closer to the ranch, he could see what was left of an outbuilding, smoldering in the distance. The house, barn, and other buildings appeared to be untouched by the blaze.

He was struck by the quiet. Even the constant drizzle that was so indicative of Florida's late summer afternoons was more like a heavy weight in the air. Cole's wide-brimmed hat almost kept him from noticing the mist.

Closer still, he saw no sign of life, no cattle, no ranch hands. He didn't think this was unusual. They might be off driving cattle to the docks in Tampa or to Titusville on the opposite coast.

Staying on his horse, Cole circled the large house with its hand-hewn cypress shingles on the roof, wraparound porch, and detached kitchen. The place looked deserted. Then he saw the woman. She was at the edge of a small orange grove leading out from the other side of the house. She was digging with a large shovel that seemed to almost overpower her. Her clothes were wet and dirty. She had drawn her long skirt and petticoats up between her legs and secured them in her belt to give her the freedom to climb in and out of the hole she was digging. As he drew closer, he could see that her face was swollen and bruised with a small bleeding cut on her chin. The woman was aware of his presence but ignored him.

She was trying to dig a grave, but the shallow hole appeared to fill up almost as fast as she shoveled out the wet sand. He got off his horse and tried to take the shovel from her hands, but soon realized that unless he wrestled her to the ground, she would not allow it.

He looked around and, near the house, he saw something wrapped in a muddy quilt under an oak. When he got closer, despite the rain, he could see that she had dragged it from the house. He squatted down and lay open the quilt. He saw the face of a man with a bullet hole in his forehead.

Catherine Hamilton didn't know she was in shock. Something in her mind, something totally out of her control, had taken over. It was as if she had split into two separate people—one mortally wounded, ready to lie down and die; the other, super energized, knowing only that this man she had loved must be buried and then vindicated. She seemed to be outside her body, looking on, as she dug the grave.

The woman continued to ignore him. Her eyes were on her work, but she looked at once crazed and detached. As Cole approached her, he began softly singing an old Charles Wesley hymn, *Thou hidden source of calm repose, thou all sufficient love divine...* She turned and gave him an incredulous look. With that, he gently but firmly pried her hands from the shovel and guided her to the base of the tree where he sat her down. Then, grabbing the shovel with his strong, leathery hands, he continued the work himself. Every so often he asked her a question.

"Is that your husband, ma'am?"

"Can you tell me what happened here?"

But the woman was silent.

Eventually the rain stopped. Together they dragged the body to the edge of the opening. The woman opened the quilt and kissed the dead man on the mouth. Then they lowered the body into the grave.

Cole began shoveling the dirt back into the hole. The woman walked to the barn and came back with a large gardening trowel.

She squatted on the ground and began filling the grave with great scoops. When they were finished, they walked to the barn and placed the tools inside.

The woman finally spoke, "You can sleep in the bunkhouse and use the kitchen, but if you try to come into the house, I will shoot you and then shoot myself."

Then she turned and walked inside.

CHAPTER TWO

COLE & ELIJAH

• • •

C ole climbed back on his horse. He rode around the barn and saw singed boards on one side but no serious fire damage. *The rain must have quenched the fire before it could take hold.* After unsaddling and feeding his horse, he went to the large, detached kitchen, stoked up the massive fireplace, made coffee, and boiled grits.

 Houses in the south traditionally had detached kitchens, so that heat from cooking was kept from the main house.

He thought of taking something to the woman, but then remembered her warning. Cole believed she really would shoot him.

He went back to the bunkhouse, took a small, ragged Bible from his saddlebag, lit a lantern, and began reading from the Old Testament. Cole's daddy had taught him as a child to read his Bible every night, telling him it would give him comfort. He had continued to do it even now, and did--on occasion--receive comfort, but not for the reasons his daddy envisioned. Cole liked reading about the prophet

Elijah because he could relate to the emotional ups and downs. Even though Elijah was called the "Troubler" of Israel, he just as well could have been called the "Troubled." And so could Cole. He read the story about the stand-off between Elijah and the other prophets and how Elijah challenged them to a kind of ultimate barbecue. Cole smiled when he came to the part where the bad prophets could not get a fire going, but God blessed Elijah so that the fire burned the wood, cooked the meat, parched the stones, and even dried up the water. Elijah was so energized that he ran a few miles to deliver the message. But Cole knew that in the next story Elijah would be so down in the dumps he'd want to die. Cole could relate to both of Elijah's moods but felt strangely calmed as he blew out the lantern and went to sleep.

The sound of a buckboard wagon rolling into the barnyard woke him with a start. It was long before daylight. He looked out one of the windows lining the bunkhouse to see a man and a woman sitting on the wagon, the man still holding the horses' reins. Finally, tentatively, the man climbed down and assisted the woman to the ground. They both seemed to be unsure about which way to go. As best he could see in the moonlight, the couple looked scared to death.

Cole came out of the bunkhouse with his hands at his side.

"Who are you?" he said.

"Who are you, mister?" the other man said.

"I'm just passing through, and the woman said I could spend the night here."

As Cole slowly walked closer, he could see the man was a Negro and the woman, a Seminole. This did not surprise Cole, as he was well aware of what had transpired over the previous five decades.

During the Seminole War years of the 1830s and continuing long after Florida won statehood in 1845, as much as half of Florida's population lived under slavery. Some Seminoles kept Africans as their slaves, while other slaves, runaways, lived among the Seminoles as allies and even warriors. The blacks who fought by the sides of the Seminoles were called "Negro-Indians." As time went on, friendships erased any differences between the groups we now refer to as Native Americans and African Americans.

After the Civil War, Gen. Sherman issued a field order authorizing the use of abandoned land in Florida for exclusive settlement by blacks. Each freed family was to be given 40 acres, clothing, seed, and farm equipment. For the most part, this didn't happen but, in many areas, it caused the Indians and the blacks to form an even closer alliance. And that, of course, resulted in more intimate relationships.

The black man looked at Cole and said, "Where's Sam Hamilton?"

"He's dead," Cole replied. The couple's faces showed grief, but not surprise.

Cole asked their names. The man was called Joe Black. The Seminole woman's name was Naomi.

CHAPTER THREE

NAOMI & JOE BLACK

• • •

Cole stayed three days. He and Joe Black cleared the debris from the burned out stable and did the other chores that needed doing while the ranch hands were off on the cattle drive. During that time, he never saw the woman.

On the second day as they were dragging charred beams to the edge of the woods, Cole finally felt it was the right time to ask Joe Black what had happened.

It was obvious to Cole that Joe Black was feeling pain as he tried to find the words to explain something so awful, something that he really didn't understand. He told Cole that he and Naomi had stayed behind when all the other ranch hands had left on the cattle drive. Because a group of bankers and investors in town wanted the ranch, at the last minute Sam Hamilton had decided to stay home himself.

Joe Black continued, "The last few days, those men really put the pressure on. Mr. Sam wasn't feelin' a bit good about leavin' Miss Catherine behind to deal with them by herself. But I know Mr. Sam really looked forward to the drive."

Cole knew that Sam Hamilton was one of the legions of well-to-do, educated northeasterners, who longed to be a part of taming America's frontier. But, like many of them, he was woefully naive about the inherent dangers he would have to confront.

Joe didn't explain why he and Naomi had disappeared for two days and Cole didn't ask.

CHAPTER FOUR

I Know Who You Are

• • •

On Cole's fourth day at the Hamilton's ranch, he stepped into the kitchen as he had the mornings before to eat the big breakfast Naomi had ready for him. This morning she had fixed fat strips of bacon, eggs fried in the bacon drippings, grits, biscuits with sweet butter and strawberry jam, sour oranges, and coffee.

As Cole turned to take his place at the table, he saw the woman sitting in the rocking chair that faced the fireplace. There was a long-nosed pistol resting in her lap. Cole started to turn and walk out of the kitchen, but she said, "Wait, I want to talk to you."

She knew who Coleman Wills was. As a writer, she had been fascinated by the stories she had heard about the legendary Wills. People in and around Orange County thought of Cole as a tough, quiet loner with an uncanny ability to heal relationships between ranchers and farmers, between Indians and white men, and even between husbands and wives. It was said that he also had a gift for physical healing. Just a few months before, Catherine had talked to a woman in town who told her that Cole Wills had delivered twins to a woman camped on the shore of the St. Johns River. Even the Methodists had trusted him for his brief but failed stint as a circuit-riding preacher. The Methodist lady who talked to Catherine had said, "At least he came out of it alive." Circuit riders were seen as heroes all across the South and the West. It was a hard life and most of them didn't live to be old men.

And she also had heard about Wills' dark side. He had a bad temper. And he sometimes disappeared for months, only to surface again—usually at some rancher's house at dinnertime.

Catherine was wearing a robe several sizes too large for her small frame. Around her shoulders was a blanket. Her hair, which had been knotted on top of her head when he first saw her, was flowing down her back and around her shoulders. He was uncomfortable seeing her in this intimate setting.

"Please sit down, Mr. Wills. I want to discuss something with you," Catherine said, as she motioned to the chair on the other side of the fireplace.

As he pulled the other rocking chair closer to the fire, he said, "How are you feeling, Mrs. Hamilton?"

She ignored the question.

She shifted in the rocker but continued to let the gun lay across her legs.

"I know who you are."

This did not surprise Cole. He knew that gossip and exaggerated stories preceded him most everywhere he went.

"I know who you are too, ma'am."

CHAPTER FIVE

Things Are Different Here
• • •

Sam Hamilton, a high-born, over educated northerner, and his fiery wife had arrived in Orange County with enough money to pay cash for their ranch and everything else they needed. So, naturally, the Hamiltons immediately were disliked by most of the other ranchers. But Catherine slowly won them over by her willingness to listen to their stories and her genuine eagerness to learn their ways. She also had a great sense of humor about who she was and where she came from. She actually had been able to strike up a spark of a relationship with their nearest neighbors, the Wilsons. She had ridden to their ranch one day to ask if their oldest daughter could do some sewing for her. Mrs. Wilson was reluctant but the daughter, Emma, a fine seamstress, wanted to do it, and in the end they relented. Catherine and Emma became fast friends and that helped thaw out the rest of the family.

One afternoon, Catherine went out to the back porch to share a cool fruit drink with Naomi. It was wash day and Naomi was just finishing up. She had started at daylight by carrying in spring water from the outside trough. Then she heated the water on the wood-burning stove. When it was hot, she poured it into a cradle-like washing machine, built by Joe Black. Constructed on a half circle, the machine had slats through the bottom and a piece of wood that could be rocked back and forth to agitate the clothes. The next day she would use several flat irons by heating them in the fireplace to finish the task.

As Catherine went around the corner of the porch, she discovered a burlap bag, filled with some sort of vegetable. She knew Emma's mother must have sent it over with Emma but what Catherine didn't know, even after she opened the bag and looked inside, was exactly what was in it. At first, she thought it might be green beans, but the pods were too dark and dry and when she tried to break them, little beans fell out. So she sat on the porch and shelled the entire bag before Naomi returned from hanging the clothes in the yard. At that moment, Emma stepped out from the living room, having worked all afternoon at the treadle sewing machine. Still not sure of what she had, Catherine looked at the pot full of beans. She saw that each one of the gray beans had a black spot on one side. All at once she shouted out loud, "They must be black-eyed peas!" Both Naomi and Emma exploded with giggles at this "city woman's" discovery. That night, Naomi served the peas after having cooked them all afternoon in the pot with a fist-sized piece of fat back. They were delicious. After Naomi explained that "fat back" was "a big ol' piece of fat bacon," Catherine carefully wrote a thank-you note on her fine Boston stationery and gave the note to Emma to deliver to her mother. That was the beginning of Catherine's and her "naturally aristocratic" husband's acceptance into the community.

Mrs. Wilson sent word to Catherine and Sam the first week in November, inviting them to a Saturday picnic at the clearing behind the two-room schoolhouse just north of Oconee. When Catherine received the invitation, she felt in her heart that she and her family had, indeed, finally been accepted.

She didn't dare trust herself to decide what to take so she asked Naomi to prepare what she thought would be the right dish for the pitch-in dinner. For the Hamiltons, meals in Central Florida were an entirely new adventure. And while Sam loved the country cooking, Catherine never really got used to it. First, she didn't eat much and that in itself made her stand out from the "Cracker" community. Also, ever since her untimely trip to town on hog-butchering day, she had declared herself a virtual vegetarian.

It had been a chilly day in December when Catherine turned the corner to meet Joe Black after having bought yard goods at the general store. There, in the field in front of her was a crudely made pen holding several squealing hogs. And just beyond that, to Catherine's distress, were two slaughtered hogs, each hanging on a kind of tripod. Catherine was both repelled and enticed by this site. She tried to tell herself that it was the writer within who nudged her forward to investigate this country ritual. She could see that the tripods had been made by driving two strong poles into the ground several feet apart and then topping them with a much longer pole. But this wasn't the worst sight. To the right, she saw two men hauling a dead hog out of a trough filled with boiling water. A log chain had been placed in the water so that the men could easily turn and lift the hog. The men placed the hog on a third tripod and began scraping hair from its body. Just then, Catherine heard a loud bang and turned to see that another man had just shot one of the hogs right between the eyes. And, before she could turn away, another man slit the hog's throat, and after letting run out what looked like gallons of blood, he cut the boar open all the way down its front and proceeded to remove its entrails.

Although Catherine was repulsed, she was strangely fascinated by the whole scene—especially the party atmosphere. Children were running and playing "shoot the hog" using sticks as guns and several happily singing women were standing at a large outdoor tub where they were cooking over an open fire. As Catherine edged closer she could see they were making lard from the hog's fat. But they could have been at a quilting bee, for all the laughter and excited chattering.

As she walked around the area, Catherine tried to discern her feelings. She understood intellectually that this was a necessary part of life, and she could even admire the fact that there was no waste. It looked as if every part of the hog was put to use. But she had a hard time with the pleasure and fun aspect, especially the obvious elite standing of the man who got to shoot the hogs. But even her own husband enjoyed hunting, so she allowed as how this couldn't be a matter of right and wrong. Perhaps it had more to do with lifestyles that she had never experienced and therefore could not appreciate. So, when one of the women invited her to join them at the fire, she thought possibly she could make herself take part in the fun for a while. But just then, she saw a dog running toward her with what looked like a bunch of snakes in his mouth. As he got closer, Catherine could see he was dangling a mouthful of intestines. Immediately she turned on her heels, beckoned Joe Black, and rushed off home.

On the cool Saturday afternoon of the picnic, Joe Black hitched up the buggy, and Catherine and Naomi carefully loaded the five fruit pies Naomi had baked. They smelled so good that Sam wasn't sure he could make it to the picnic without eating one.

Catherine had invited Naomi and Joe Black to go to the picnic with them. Her whole life, Catherine had had difficulty separating classes of people. Despite her Boston education, she had a democratic heart. She couldn't separate the teaching, "All are acceptable in God's sight," from the realities of who would acceptable at a cracker picnic. But Naomi and Joe Black knew better and, shaking their heads as if to say, "When will this woman learn what's what?" they declined the invitation.

Catherine and Sam had a good time at the picnic. The women brought baskets of fried chicken, squirrel and rabbit, plus biscuits and cornbread. Some brought cured venison, bear meat, and bacon.

Salt was among the early settlers' primary methods of preserving meat. Families stored salted pork, beef, venison, fish, and rabbit in barrels, sealing out air with layers of lard. Florida's humidity was too high to rely on the sun to dry most foods. Smoked and salted meats could keep for a year or more, but every housewife had a private store of tricks for disguising the taste and smell of dubious pieces. Most cracker wives cooked their meals outdoors. In the summertime, they often cooked the full day's meals before dawn to avoid doing the cooking chores in the heat of the day. Tomatoes and greens were brought in from the garden. Green beans were strung and cooked for hours with salted pork. Squash and onions were fried in the fat from the chicken, and butter was churned. When it was available, tea was boiled in a large pan on the stove and sugar was added while it was still simmering. Sometimes the biscuits were split, and pieces of fried, home-cured ham were inserted.

This was October and the days were getting cooler—the perfect time to be in Florida was upon them. At the picnic, there were great quantities of greens, corn, pickles, and other vegetables, plus pies and cakes. Long before the gathering, chickens were killed and "dressed," drenched in flour, salt and pepper, and fried in cast iron skillets. The women did all the work, while the men and children played.

The women dragged an old scrubbed-up laundry kettle into the middle of the clearing where a fire had been laid. The kettle was filled with fat and, after it started to bubble, fresh-caught fish were deep-fried. Along with them, savory corn dodgers were cooked in the same fat. Sam thought they were as light and delectable as anything he had eaten on the continent.

Toward the end of the afternoon, a few of the men went to a wagon and came back with some cane beer they had just brought from a trip to the sugar cane area around the little community of Bell in North Florida. This potent brew was the hot cane juice that was skimmed off the boiling syrup and sugar and then left to ferment.

The syrup itself was a delight to the taste buds served on biscuits or, for some people, served on just about anything. But the cane beer had a peculiar sour or fermented taste. The women and some of the men were not at all happy that this brew was being consumed at the picnic, and they scooted the children away as the group of men sat under the tall pines at the edge of the clearing enjoying themselves.

It was a fine afternoon with games and singing around the fish kettle and nonstop eating. As dusk approached and people began to pack up their belongings for the long trip home, Catherine was feeling even better about their acceptance into the community than she did when the invitation came. Sam called to her that it was time to go, so she found her way around the dessert end of the makeshift tables to gather her pie tins. But as she looked at the table, her heart sank. Four of the five pies had not been touched. She knew Sam had most likely eaten the one slice missing from the fifth pie. Furious, she found Mrs. Wilson to try to get some sort of explanation. Her first thought was that these crackers were refusing to eat food prepared by her Seminole housekeeper, but she wondered how they would even know that Naomi had made the pies. But Mrs. Wilson set her straight saying, "crackers don't eat food fixed by Yankees."

CHAPTER SIX

20 Years Earlier

• • •

For as long as people have been on the earth, life has never been the same after a war. Cole had been 12 years old when his daddy came home all battered and so thin he could barely keep his clothes on his body. But, unlike some of their neighbors, Arthur Wills was a grateful man.

In 1864, after three mean years of fighting, Arthur had been with a rag tag group of Floridians in the woods south of Savannah, when Sherman left a burned-out Atlanta and proceeded on his march to the sea.

The Federal troops marched through Savannah like a mighty twister, turning the city and its residents upside down. They utterly destroyed everything in their path, including the railroads. Millionaires were turned into paupers overnight. On December 22nd Sherman wired a message to President Lincoln, *I beg to present you as a Christmas gift the city of Savannah, with 150 heavy guns and plenty of ammunition, also about 25 thousand bales of cotton.*

Confederate soldiers were often referred to as rebels, or "rebs" and sometimes as Johnny Rebs.

The Reb officers had fled days before, but the word didn't reach men like Arthur Wills until it was too late. To Arthur's eye, it seemed all so senseless, since there was no longer resistance to the Union. The men lay in the woods for two days, covered with bugs and muck, until they thought it was safe to start their walk back to Florida. Then, they traveled at night and tried to find safe places to sleep during the day. There was very little food to be found. They foraged for berries and looked for game, though there was no way to start a fire. And even if there had been a way, they wouldn't have dared draw attention to themselves.

When Arthur Wills had volunteered and left his wife and son to fight in this war, he never in his worst nightmare could have imagined what it would be like. He had understood that dying was a possibility, but he'd envisioned an honorable death on the battlefield. He wasn't alone in his misperceptions.

Imprinted on Arthur's mind for the rest of his life would be the sight of young boys in Confederate uniforms camped in the woods—crying and sucking their thumbs in the night.

Despite the fact that both sides instituted conscription–the draft– both armies were overwhelmingly composed of volunteers. But it was not only a volunteer's war; it also was a children's war. Ten to 20 percent of the confederate soldiers were underage. Drummer boys and buglers were sometimes no older than 12 or 13.

The Civil War also was a brother's war—fratricide at the highest degree. Every Confederate state except South Carolina sent regiments into both the union and Confederate armies, with brother fighting against brother.

A year and a day after Arthur joined up, he and another soldier, Zebedee Baylou were trying to find their way back to camp from a scouting expedition. Both Floridians, they hunkered down in their coats as they crossed a railroad bridge. Neither man had ever before felt such a powerful wind rip through his body. With little effect, they hunched against it. All day long, they'd seen dead soldiers lying where they had been killed—some dressed in blue, others in gray. By late afternoon, the sight of decaying bodies stirred no emotion in either of them.

During the war, the railroad bridges were destroyed and rebuilt with prefabricated segments known as "shad-belly" trusses. Both armies went to great strides to keep their supply routes open, as trains bringing food and medicine were all that kept whole battalions alive. And yet, both sides also were good at tearing down railroad tracks and bridges.

When they reached the end of the bridge Zeb squinted his eyes, as he peered into the ravine some 100 feet down the side of the overpass. All at once he took off in a dead-run down the hill. Stumbling, he got upright without slowing his pace and then skidded, tumbling part of the way down. Arthur followed, thinking Zeb noticed something worth stealing from one of the several gray-clad bodies lying on the creek's shore below.

Stealing from corpses was common war practice. In the beginning, men took on what they needed—boots or guns—but, as the war dragged on, it was common to see a body stripped clean.

Arthur had never stolen from the dead because he had promised his wife, Stine, he wouldn't do anything in the war that would make his son ashamed of him. She had prepared Arthur to keep his promise, by making sure he had heavy long woolen underwear and the finest boots she could find in Apopka City.

Zeb knelt next to the corpse of a boy, not more than 16 years old, and began sobbing. Reaching his arms around the boy's back, he tried to lift him but the body was stiff. He cradled the boy in his arms, crooning over and over, "Oh, baby boy, baby boy…"

Arthur squatted, rocked back on his heels for a few seconds to size up the situation, and then gently tried to pull Zeb away from the body.

"Who is he, Corporal," Arthur asked compassionately. Shaking uncontrollably, Zeb answered, "He's my baby brother."

Still trying to guide Zeb away from the boy's body, Arthur said, "My God, man! How can that be? It don't make no sense."

With tears streaming down his dirty face, Zeb looked up at Arthur and said, "He's 10 years younger 'en me, so we had different ideas about the war, but I loved my baby brother. Because he came along so late, Ma called him 'baby boy,' 'til he got tired of it and made her stop. But he was jus' a baby and now he's dead."

That night, after burying the boy, Arthur and Zeb staggered into camp around sunset. They made their report, omitting the part about Zeb's little brother, and then they both lay down on the ground to sleep. Exhausted, Arthur had conflicted feelings about the war for the first time.

As Arthur drifted off, he thanked God for Stine and little Cole. Then, he asked God to give him back the conviction that he was fighting a just and holy battle. But it was not to be. Around 4:00 a.m., he woke up to find a man from his own company tugging at his boots. As he sat up, the man smashed him in the head with the butt of a handgun.

Although he saved his boots, the foolish attempt a desperate comrade made to warm his feet resulted in Arthur's first experience in a field hospital—two years prior to the fall of Savannah.

CHAPTER SEVEN

BLOODY HELL

• • •

To contract a disease or be wounded in the Civil War was a virtual death sentence, and certainly not a quick and clean death. Casualties of the war were doomed to die slowly and in agony. For the Rebels, almost two out of three would not return home alive.

The usual kind of battlefield medical procedure during the war consisted almost exclusively of amputation. The most popular doctors were those whose coats were the bloodiest. This meant they were fast. At best, the most these expectant amputees could hope for was a quick and clean cut.

Although chloroform and ether were widely used in big cities, the anesthesia of choice in the battlefield was whiskey. But even liquor wasn't always available. Those who didn't die from shock often developed erysipelas, (an especially virulent form of staph infection), or already were so weak from malnutrition or disease that they lived a few agonizing days and then died.

Arthur had spent a week in the field hospital with his head wrapped in a dirty bandage, the wound resulting from the boot incident. From his vantage spot on a cot outside the surgical tent, he could see that the doctor was drinking most of the brandy and whiskey that occasionally arrived in the camp before it ever reached anybody else. As far as Arthur could tell, the doctor was drunk most of the time. Consequently, even though he was a skilled surgeon, the man had a cruel and brutal indifference to the needs of the men.

For the week he was there, Arthur watched the surgeon use the same dirty sea sponge to clean wound after wound. And even though he had an array of surgical tools available, the doctor used his finger almost exclusively as a probe. He would go from one patient to the next, using the same blood-dripping finger and surgical saw. His clothes reeked with human innards. Later, Arthur would tell his friends that he felt lucky his injury was to his head because it couldn't be amputated.

When Arthur's wound had healed enough for him to stand up, he pulled on his boots and promptly left the camp to find his unit.

The Reb officers had fled days before but the word didn't reach men like Author until it was too late. They lay in the woods for days, covered with bugs and muck, until they thought it was safe to start their own way back to Florida.

Trying to stay out of sight, they worked their way through trails in the thick forest. They foraged for berries and looked for game even though they had no way of starting a fire and wouldn't have dared draw the attention to themselves even if they did. There was very little food to be found.

This time, though, on the fifth night after escaping from the Savannah woods, Arthur and his straggly group of fellow soldiers stumbled upon a Reb medical station. The men were all suffering from starvation, dehydration, and a fever of unknown source. Even so, Arthur was about to have an experience that would change his life and the life of his son forever.

Just before they got to the campsite, Arthur had passed out. When he woke up from the delirium that had possessed him for almost a week, six days had passed since the others had dragged him into this safe haven. An old woman was pressing a wet rag to his head. He knew then and there that this was unlike any medical camp he had known or heard about since the war began. Over the next few days, his life would be transformed by the good that took place in this little refuge from the madness of the closing months of the war. While many of the Civil War medical corps were poorly trained and some were just soldiers who were good with their hands, the doctor at this camp was a brilliant, educated man from Emory University named Nathan Harlow. He was a devout Methodist who saw this war as not only an opportunity to use his medical skills but also to put his theology to the test. Arthur soon fell under the spell of this man and experienced what others have described as a battlefield conversion.

When Arthur became well enough to leave, there was no place to go, as his unit had long been separated and scattered. As a result, he spent the rest of the war at the camp assisting Dr. Harlow, and his conversion continued. He later told anybody who would listen that this opportunity to stay was his "by the grace a' God!"

Many years would come and go before Arthur's son would reach manhood. And yet, Arthur had a strange sense that, like him, Cole was destined to live his life under the protection of God's grace.

CHAPTER EIGHT

An Offer Too Good
to Refuse
· · ·

C atherine's eyes were still puffy from crying tears of devastating grief and the fear, frustration, and unfairness of more loss to follow. She looked very tired to Cole as he watched her rock slowly, staring into the fire.

Finally, she said, "They're coming back on Wednesday morning. They will expect me to give them the ranch. I won't do it. I want at least $20,000, and if you will help me get it, I'll give you ten percent. That's $2,000."

CHAPTER NINE

An Evil Man

• • •

Robert Barton was a charming man. It was fortunate for him that—upon meeting him—most people could not tell the difference between charming and good. Barton was not good. He was evil.

Florida soil made Barton rich but he was neither a rancher, nor a farmer. He didn't love the land. He didn't appreciate the beauty of the flora and fauna. He didn't love the wild animals that roamed the woods and swamps or the cattle that made men wealthy. He loved neither the warm winters nor the hot, wet summers. What he loved was power.

In the land of wide-open spaces, Barton bought and sold property. There was, of course, no innate evil in this enterprise. Many of the earliest land developers like Flagler and Plant brought civilization and opportunity to early settlers. But Barton's agenda was different. In addition to his insatiable hunger for power, he delighted in wielding his power over others and making them suffer.

After he had been thrown out of a small town in Tennessee for beating a man nearly to death, Barton drifted down to Florida.

Because he made such good first impressions, he soon endeared himself to the townspeople in Oconee where he eventually settled. Every morning Barton took his breakfast at the only café in town. Anna Magby the owner's daughter, began to happily anticipate exchanging pleasantries with him as she brought his eggs and grits to the table. Eventually, the cheerful banter took on a more sinister tone, and Barton became aggressive in his attempts to get Anna to go out with him. One morning a row ensued and Anna's father threw Barton out of the café.

The next day, some alligator trappers discovered Anna in a swamp about four miles out of town. She was badly beaten and her right ear was partially sliced off.

Then a strange dichotomy emerged. Some people totally steered clear of Barton while others were exceedingly nice to him when they encountered him eating in the café, boarding his horse, or entering or exiting the boarding house.

As Barton's fortune and his whispered reputation grew, he discovered it was even easier to be intimidating than it had been before. Ranchers and businessmen in town appeared grateful for his charming, affable manner and were willing to put up with most anything from him.

Barton's usual practice was to find a ranch that was doing well, buy out the owner for cash, and then sell the ranch at a tremendous profit. He did this by intimidation, and if that did not work, he committed gross acts of brutality on the landowner.

He delighted in seeing fear and suffering in the eyes of his clients. His only regret, as his business success grew, was that he no longer had the time or the freedom to personally inflict damage. Instead, he was forced to rely on colleagues to do his dirty work.

With the railroad making its way from Jacksonville through the center of the state, Barton knew it would bring wealthy winter visitors from the north. He also knew it would bring an end to the land grabs and endless grazing lands in the area. He was behind many of the incidents of sabotage to trains that were now foraging south. It was not unusual that guns would be fired at passenger cars and entire herds of cattle would be discovered grazing on the tracks. Trains would be forced to come to screeching stops, causing breakdowns, injury to passengers, and constant delays.

Barton was firmly in control of the small town of Oconee in Northeast Orange County—the closest town to the Hamilton Ranch. He was seen, at best, as a benevolent dictator and at worst, a despot. But no one doubted his power.

CHAPTER TEN

UNEXPECTED STRENGTH

• • •

For about half a mile from the Hamilton property's entrance to the clearing, where the house stood, live oaks and other trees lined the trail. At several places along the way, the tall trees formed an enchanting arched canopy across the trail, shielding it from the sun. Before the heavy humidity and heat set in for the day, Catherine often felt as if she'd been transported back to the Garden of Eden.

Early summer mornings in Florida were beautiful in the 1800s. Foliage was lush and thick with great flowering plants. Among the most impressive was the magnolia tree. Technically, not a tree but a bush, the magnolia, nevertheless, grew to over 20 feet in height. It was beautiful all year round with great shiny leaves, but in late April and all of May—giant white blossoms, eight to 10 inches across, filled the tree from top to bottom.

Catherine loved the magnolias. She thought they had a never-changing, eternal quality—as long as they were not touched. When touched, though, the dark shiny green leaves and the exquisite flowers immediately began to turn brown. For this reason, she never picked them or any other flower on her property. Although she was not consciously aware of it, the sight of wilting flowers had made her sad, ever since her mother's death.

But on this Wednesday morning Catherine had instructed Naomi to clip a great quantity of magnolias and place them in water-filled bowls throughout the house.

At around 10:00 a.m. three men rode up the trail, through the arched canopy, to the ranch. Cole saw the dust rising from the galloping horses beyond the orange grove, as he and Joe Black worked on the final repairs to the partially burned barn. Upon their arrival, the visitors climbed down from their horses and gathered at the porch. There was Charles Landry president of the bank, and Robert Barton, who was known throughout Central Florida as a rising cattle baron. Barton was ruthless in his attempts to take over ranches and cattle, and everybody knew it.

Naomi opened the door and stood aside as the three men walked in. Terrified, she quickly backed out of the room.

Whatever the men expected wasn't what they saw when Catherine entered the room. Robert Barton would not have been surprised if she either had already packed up and headed back north (where she belonged) or cowered in a corner somewhere, too afraid to even see them. However Catherine boldly burst into the room, wearing men's riding pants and boots that had been polished to a glossy sheen. Her white shirt and fringed jacket made her look as though she was getting ready to star in the Kissimmee Rodeo.

Her magnificent hair was piled on top of her head with whips of curls circling her face. The swelling and puffiness from having been beaten around the face was all but concealed with artfully applied makeup.

Catherine *was* momentarily inwardly terrified, as the third man appeared. He was one of the men who had come to her home three days before and had changed her life forever. Her body and mind turned to stone for an instant. Then, clutching the back of a chair, she surprised herself by the strength and authority of her voice.

"Hello, Mr. Barton. What can I do for you today?"

Confused as he was by the sight of this woman when he was expecting a beaten, broken, terrified human being like the ones he had seen so many times after his men had finished with them, he pulled himself together and said,

"We've come to offer you a fair price for your ranch so you can get out of here and go on back up north where your folks can take care of you."

The three of them, still standing because she had not invited them to sit, waited for her reply. Catherine was keenly aware that there was no mention of her husband's death.

"And what might that be?" She spoke.

"I brought Charlie Landry with me so that you could have the money right away. I'm willing to give you $4,000 cash right now!

Today!"

Catherine forced a smile. The men were bewildered. *Was she demented? Had she lost her mind?*

"You know our foreman and ranch hands have driven our cattle to Tampa. Twelve hundred head. At $20 a head, they should come back with $24,000. That, plus the ranch makes this place worth at least $50,000."

Robert Barton moved forward. His eyes narrowed perceptively. "I am offering you $4,000. You can't run this ranch by yourself. Your husband was bad enough at it."

Catherine brazenly walked over to the massive mahogany side table that Sam had shipped down from Jacksonville. Somehow, the derogatory way in which this man mentioned her husband strengthened her inner resolve. She opened the decanter and poured herself a drink. She did not offer one to the three men standing in her entranceway. Just then Coleman Wills appeared from another part of the house. He didn't say anything. He walked up and stood close by but slightly behind her.

"I've been thinking about running the ranch myself, along with my old friend here. You're right. My husband made a mess of things, but that's over. Cole knows what he's doing."

At that point, the conversation became a battle of wits. The men didn't know what to think. How could they have been wrong about this silly prim and proper northern woman? After going back and forth with her for a while, the men reluctantly agreed on $20,000 cash to be delivered to Catherine the next morning at the bank. She was then to vacate the house within the week.

When the three were leaving the front porch, the third man—the one who had been there before—said within Catherine's hearing,

"I should have killed that bitch when I had the chance."

The senseless viciousness of that statement reminded Coleman Wills of the stories his father had related about the war. Although these days were considered to be *peaceful times*, man's shadow side and his capacity for evil were clearly evident to Cole.

CHAPTER ELEVEN

THE WAR
• • •

Not unlike Arthur Wills, Dr. Nathan Harlow possessed unrealistic illusions about the war being an opportunity to give the best that he had for God and country. And in his mind, the country was the Confederate States of America. He learned very quickly that, even though he had a prestigious reputation as a surgeon in Georgia, he was woefully naive about the war.

During his first two weeks in the field hospital, he was horrified to see countless arms and legs piled in a hole behind the surgical tents. One night he lay in his tent staring at the ceiling. He knew he had to make a decision or he was destined to become like the surgeon he replaced—a drunken, cynical shadow of a man, or even worse. Around 4:00 a.m. he wrote a letter to his wife:

My darling Olivia,

How many times have you told me that I am the strength of your life? But I want you to know that if it was not for the steadfast love of God and your love, my darling, I would have been destroyed by this battlefield medical unit. Everything I see around me sickens me. There is no glory in this war—only pain and suffering.

I have been in prayer for several hours and this is what has come to me. First, do you remember the story that Reverend Trembly told us when we were sitting at his dinner table last summer? He said that we alone cannot save the entire world, but we can work on cleaning up our spot in it. And as he was talking, he was clearing his dirty dishes from the table, leaving the beautiful lace tablecloth and his china cup, spoon, and saucer in perfect symmetry.

Olivia, with God's help, I am going to try, as best I can, to keep my little spot clean.

Tell Dr. Long to continue to send medical supplies to me, via our "riding friends," and remind him that we need ether more than anything else. I will try to not let anything keep me from being God's servant in mind and body. But if I should fail, please know that I tried my best.

You are constantly in my thoughts and prayers.

Your loving husband,
    Nathan

Arthur's bond with Dr. Harlow that began soon after he arrived at the camp strengthened as the weeks wore on. For the first time in his life—aside from the feelings he had for Cole—Arthur felt truly drawn to another human being. Dr Harlow had all of the qualities he yearned to embody himself. As for the lonely doctor, he was grateful to have a companion who understood, in a way, that it was important to give one's best in these miserable circumstances. Arthur's admiration reaffirmed Harlow's calling.

One night the two of them sat on a log by an open fire, trying to calm themselves after spending an exhausting afternoon caring for five broken bodies that had been dragged in by straggling Rebs, trying to find their way back home. The oldest of the casualties could not have been more than 18. Besides their considerable wounds, all of the patients had dysentery. Their bodies were caked with mud and feces, and maggots crawled from their wounds. Arthur stripped and bathed the young boys. The stench was so bad that he and the doctor were left alone in their work. Dr. Harlow began cleaning and stitching gaping holes before resorting to amputation only as a last resort. At the end of the day—despite the best efforts of the doctor and his aid—all of the injured men were dead.

The saving grace in the afternoon's carnage was ether. At least death had come with a little less pain than it would have without the anesthetic. So, while they drank thick coffee, Arthur told Dr. Harlow about his head-wound experience, and the camp doctor's inability or unwillingness to ease the pain of the dying men.

Dr. Harlow closed his eyes, as if trying to draw memories from another life. Finally he said, "For many years, I practiced medicine in Jefferson, Georgia, by the side of a great man. His name was Dr. Crawford Long. He was as much a scientist as he was a doctor, so we were always learning and experimenting. In the days before there were rumors of war, we were on the top of every Jefferson socialite's list. Dr. Crawford taught me that these parties were great places to observe human nature.

"Ether parties," as they were called by the so-called high society in Jefferson, were a case in point. In addition to downing champagne and the finest Kentucky bourbon available, inhaling ether was a common practice of the partygoers. Dr. Long watched his friends as they lost their inhibitions and danced on tabletops and chairs. One night, he stopped by my house to tell me that he had been "dumb struck" to witness a young man fall off a table, break his leg, and continue to try to dance as if nothing had happened. Dr. Long immediately knew that he had discovered what might be this century's breakthrough in pain-killing drugs for surgery.

Arthur asked, "If what you say is true, why ain't you and this Dr. Long rich and famous?"

"Well, Arthur, like a lot of compassionate men, my friend and colleague, Crawford Long, didn't publish his breakthrough finding, so it took a few more years for ether to become properly recognized and popular as a pain-killing drug."

And now—three years later in this other battlefield medical unit, deep in the forest in North Florida—to Arthur's surprise, Dr. Harlow had somehow managed to store ether to use when operating on his wounded patients. But what surprised Arthur even more was the *lack* of surgery Dr. Harlow performed.

This doctor had some bazaar ideas—especially about transferring germs from one patient to another. He insisted that Arthur and everyone else working in the camp wash their hands with fresh water as they moved from one patient to another. If, on the rare occasion the little creek running close by was not flowing and water was scarce, they were required to wipe their hands on rags. But the most remarkable thing that Arthur observed was that the doctor very seldom amputated limbs. He tried to clean wounds and keep the men comfortable. He constantly reminded Arthur and others of the Hippocratic Oath as they were standing over a mangled body: *First, do no harm...* And then he sometimes would remind them of the obvious—that after three years in the war, common sense was telling him that chopping off limbs, only to watch a man die in inconceivable agony, seemed to be quite harmful.

CHAPTER TWELVE

SAD GOODBYES BACK AT THE RANCH

• • •

C atherine knew what the banker and his friends fully intended to do to her. To say that they would cause her harm would be an understatement.

As soon as the men were out of sight, Catherine called Naomi and Joe Black into the kitchen. She told them they must pack up and leave for good. She told Joe Black to get out the big buckboard and load up anything he wanted. She told Naomi to pack all the food and supplies from the kitchen that they could carry and be ready to leave that afternoon. She spent the rest of the day thinking and planning with Cole and saying goodbye to the things she loved in her home.

That evening she went out behind the outbuilding to the fresh dirt under the Live Oak and said goodbye to her beloved Sam.

When Joe Black and Naomi were loaded up and sitting on the buckboard, Naomi crying and rolling her apron in her fingers, Catherine hugged them both and stuffed a wad of bills in Joe Black's shirt pocket. And then she watched them drive off, knowing she would never see them again.

CHAPTER THIRTEEN

A NEW LIFE

• • •

Cole's unique abilities as a healer could not all be attributed to his dad, as his mother, Ernestine Wills, was a strong, fearless Florida pioneer in her own right. When she married Arthur Wills, if she had known what a hard, solitary life was ahead, she might have chosen another path. In fact, she often told Arthur, "It's a good thing the good Lord doesn't let us see into the future because most of us couldn't take it."

Referred to as *Stine* by her friends and family, Ernestine was married her whole adult life, and she and Cole's father died within 24 hours of each other. But, like many pioneer women, she was essentially alone most of that time. She made as good a life for herself and her boy—and her husband, whenever he showed up— as she could under the circumstances. But, as she rhetorically asked Cole years later, "What other choice did I have?"

Stine was tall and physically strong, and the Florida heat and humidity seemed to make her stronger rather than deplete her. She ran the small ranch just outside of Apopka City as well as any man could have. Her body was muscular and her skin was brown and leathery from working in the sun most of the year.

Cole's mother and father never had slaves, but there was a black family living in a shack on the property for as long as he could remember, and the younger children of that family were Cole's playmates when he was a child. The older boys were black cowboys who roamed the range and drove the small herd to the coast every year. If Cole's dad wasn't around to help, Cole and his mother rode with them.

Stine oversaw the ranch, milked the farm cows, tended the garden, and preserved vegetables, fruits, and meats; raised chickens, ran an orderly house, and, in general, kept the family afloat financially. But the thing about his mom Cole remembered most was that she was a midwife. When word would come that a baby was on the way, Stine would grab her old bag, fill it with a bottle of carbolic acid, a pair of scissors, a needle and thread, hydrogen peroxide, some strips of old cloth, a knife, and a ball of string.

She quickly would go to the barn, hitch her cracker pony up to the buggy, lift Cole into the seat, and off they would go.

Most of the time, she didn't have to do much while overseeing a birth. As she said, "The woman having the baby does all the work. That why it's called labor."

One afternoon Stine and Cole traveled to a farm some 10 miles away. While Cole was playing in the yard with the boy who earlier that day had come to fetch them, Stine called out to him from the porch.

"Cole, come here. James, you stay where you are."

The boy James did as he was told. He didn't want to see his momma writhing in pain like she had when he'd left her earlier in the day. Cole felt small and scared when he stepped into the house. He'd never before been invited inside when the birthing was going on. Stine took him by the shoulders and said, "Cole, remember last spring when you and dad were birthing cows and you had to help that calf come into the world?"

Cole nodded with a look of terror on his face. He knew what was coming next.

"Well, Cole, you have to help me do this for Mrs. Scharr. The baby is stuck, and she is too weak and tired to push it out. So, you and I are going to pull it out."

Cole continued to look terrified.

Stine said, "I know you can do this!"

Cole walked into the little bedroom with his mother. White as the wet pillow she was lying on, Mrs. Scharr was perspiring heavily and staring at the ceiling.

Stine took Cole's hand and said, "Don't think about anything but getting this baby out."

Stine parted the women's knees. All Cole could see between Mrs. Scharr's legs was a large round, wet, hairy object.

"Mrs. Scharr is too tired to push much, so the next time her pain comes, I want you to help me gently pull this baby out. Do you think you can do that, Cole?"

He just looked at his mother, dumbfounded. About a minute later, Mrs. Scharr began to moan, appearing to be at death's door. The hairy ball started to move slightly and, all at once, it became a face. "Now, Cole!" Stine shouted.

And to Cole's amazement, Stine reached inside. She got her small hands around the baby's shoulders and Cole managed to get his hands around his mother's wrists. Together they pulled the baby free. Stine wiped out the baby's mouth with her finger, and after the tiny being sputtered and gave out a weak cry, Stine put the baby into Mrs. Scharr's arms.

"Alright, go wash your hands at the pump and then you can go back to the yard. Tell James he has a baby brother."

Stine and Cole stayed the night, and Mr. Scharr arrived from Gainesville the next morning. He was surprised to see his new son—small, but healthy, nursing at the breast of his exhausted, happy wife.

In the days that followed, Cole felt exhilarated. He didn't understand it, but he knew that, so far, helping with this birth was the most important thing that he had done in his young life.

CHAPTER FOURTEEN

GETTIN' AN EDUCATION

• • •

A fter Arthur came home from the war, Stine nursed him back to health. When he was strong again, he went off to be an itinerant preacher in the Methodist Church.

When Florida was opened to Protestantism in 1821, the Methodists came to the area. Methodist and Baptist circuit riders typically followed pioneer trails south and out west into new settlements. As it was for the pioneers, the life of a circuit rider on the trail was very hard.

Arthur Wills, now Rev. Wills, was the traveling Methodist preacher for eight Florida communities with official church sites on the northern end of the Orlando circuit. Betwixt and between, he attended little worship gatherings of friends and neighbors who were too far from official congregations to be part of them. All in all, he made about 17 stops as he traveled on horseback the 50-mile circuit through the wilderness.

Arthur was on the trail almost all the time, riding from settlement to settlement. Cole went along on many trips. Otherwise, he seldom would have seen his father. Time and time again, Cole's mother was left behind to live her life alone at the ranch.

In the evenings, Arthur told Cole stories about the war and about his ideas about illness and healing. He always would say to Cole when he started such discussions, "Healin' is a different thing from curin'."

Some nights, he would read from John Wesley's "Primitive Physick," an essay from the 1700s on natural methods for curing most diseases. Wesley, a renowned theologian living in the 18th century squalor of London, wrote the book because he had decidedly unorthodox ideas on a number of social issues, including medicine. Dr. Harlow had given Arthur his old, tattered copy of the book when they parted.

Arthur told Cole, "At a time when folks would kill for a piece of meat and a pint of ale, Wesley was tellin' 'em to eat vegetables and drink water."

Cole's eyelids would get heavy, and he would drift off to sleep listening to his daddy read from the book:

To prevent swelling from a bruise, immediately apply a cloth five or six times, doubled, dip in cold water... For a head cold, pare very thin yellow rind of an orange. Roll it up inside out and thrust a roll into each nostril.

Cole grew up knowing the Central Florida area like the back of his hand–every trail, every marshland, and every settlement. But as time went on it was hard for him to keep up, due to the popularity of the area.

In the late 1800s new settlements began to spring up throughout Central Florida. Orlando was a cowtown and the largest ranches in the state were around a little community south of Orlando called Kissimmee. At that time, more cattle were still raised in Florida than in any other state. In fact, civilization came to Florida because the environment was ideal for cattle raising. Central Florida also became a popular location for farming settlements, and crops could be grown all year long.

When Cole was in his teens, his mother insisted that he come off the trail, settle down, and take his studies seriously. His dad reluctantly agreed. Both parents viewed education as a high priority. Arthur hoped that Cole would follow in his footsteps to become a Methodist preacher. However, he wanted him to get an education as a *real* preacher, like they had in the big cities. Cole went through the 12th grade in the little three-room schoolhouse five miles from their home. Then, through a series of events prompted only by his parents' intense desire for Cole to have an education, he was sent to a new Methodist college in Orlando called the Florida Institute.

Although Cole had no idea what he wanted to do, he did know he wanted to do it outdoors. However, to his surprise, he enjoyed studying philosophy and religion. He especially liked learning more about his daddy's hero, John Wesley. Wesley truly cared about people and seemed to embody the values Cole's father had passed down to him. However, Wesley was a strange, solitary man, who had a tough time opening up with those close to him. This described Cole's daddy to a T. Later on it also would describe Cole, as well.

Cole had long embraced Wesley's ideas about healing. Now he was further inspired by learning that Wesley had been thrown out of the Church of England for his beliefs. He had ridden on horseback from village to village across the English countryside, preaching on the hillsides and in front of taverns. Many times he was beaten up and thrown back on his horse, only to travel to the next village, where he would do it all over again.

One night Cole's loud laughter woke up his roommates as he was reading in Mr. Wesley's journal: *...as the mob closely attended us, throwing in the windows...whatever came next to hand. But a large gentlewoman who sat in my lap screened me, so that nothing came near me.*

Cole learned something else at the institute. He learned to gamble. Late at night, he and his classmates would gather in the woods to play cards and drink gin. Cole liked playing poker, and he was good at it. It made him feel alive and sure of himself. When he was winning, the happy and gregarious Cole could stay awake for days on end.

When Cole had won about all he could from the college boys, he went to Orlando to gamble. At first, the men at the Armadillo Saloon wouldn't allow him in the game but when they saw the kind of stakes he laid out right before their eyes, they changed their minds and welcomed the green college kid to their game.

One night, while playing a game of five-card stud at the Armadillo Salon, Cole won $2,500. If he'd had the opportunity, he probably would have lost it the very next night. However, the school authorities had discovered the college boys' late-night card playing. And because Cole had taken his winnings from the other students with him, they were eager to talk about Cole's escapades in Orlando. The very next day, the college sent Cole home in disgrace. He was 19 years old.

CHAPTER FIFTEEN

UNTETHERED

• • •

Cole worked for a while as a ranch hand in Kissimmee. Later he used his Armadillo Saloon gambling earnings to purchase a 5,000-acre ranch in north Orange County. Unfortunately for Cole, he lost the ranch in a card game a few months later.

In 1871 both of his parents died in the smallpox outbreak. Devastated by the loss, Cole barely spoke for six months.

Despite his ups and downs Cole was back where he had grown up, on the land he loved. He roamed around his beloved countryside, hunting deer in the forest and fishing in the tea-colored waters of the St. Johns River.

Everybody knew Cole and he was well liked by most everybody. Even though he didn't talk much, he was able to help folks settle their differences by talking through their problems. He even worked for a time as a deputy sheriff in Apopka City and he was good at it.

CHAPTER SIXTEEN

THE METHODISTS

• • •

By the late 1870s the Methodist Church had established meeting places all over Florida, but preachers were hard to come by. Some Methodists built churches, some met in homes, and some sat around campfires. They were strung together in circuits so they could share a preacher. The Apopka Circuit consisted of Apopka City, Altamonte, Maitland, Starke Lake, Tildens, Mt. Pisgah, Salem, and Conquest. The preacher traveled on horseback to visit each parish in the circuit on a regular basis. Along with conducting Sunday services, he would visit in homes and do what he could for the parishioners before traveling on. The death of a circuit rider was not unusual, as the preachers regularly encountered hardships on the trail. Accidents, sickness, and danger were part of the job. In fact, when the first annual meeting for the Methodist Church in America was established in Philadelphia in the Lovely Lane Church in 1784 the first hymn they sang was "And Are We Yet Alive?" It's still sung to this day as the first hymn at every annual conference of the Methodist Church.

At this point in time, the rider for the Apopka Circuit was a man named Joshua Ben Stevens. One evening about dusk, Mr. Stevens went to visit a family of new parishioners at Starke Lake Parish at the eastern edge of the circuit. He had been given the word that the entire family had come down with yellow fever and the baby had died. Unfortunately, Mr. Stevens rode up the wrong path.

Brad Bixby, the owner of a fern and celery farm saw the rider from his cabin window. Half crazy with yellow fever himself he mistook Mr. Stevens for another in a long line of swindlers trying to cheat him out of his farm. He shot the preacher dead as he climbed off his horse.

The presiding elder, whose job it was to find and appoint preachers for the area, knew Cole and went to him with a request. Would Cole replace the circuit rider temporarily, until a permanent replacement could be found? Cole protested that he had no credentials and, more important, he was "…the kind of man a preacher should be savin', not the other way around."

Actually, Cole had never doubted the existence of God. But he was familiar with what was in the Bible and found many of God's decisions to be questionable, even reprehensible. He did not, however, mention this opinion during the meeting.

The next week the presiding elder visited Cole again and asked, "Do you believe all those things your daddy taught you?"

"Yeah, I guess," Cole mumbled. Then the PE asked, "Is there anything going on in your life right now so's to embarrass the church?" Cole's response was, "Well, not at the present time."

"Then you can do it. Besides, there's nobody else. It's you or nothing. These people respect you. They need you," the PE asserted.

So, Cole began his career as a Methodist supply pastor—a career that would last a little less than a year. He was not a good preacher. He had a low, unpleasant voice, and even when he had something special to say—which wasn't very often—people had trouble hearing him. He generally read the scripture and quoted things he had heard his daddy say from the pulpit years before.

Cole spent much of the time on his beloved trails, as he traveled from parish to parish. He was familiar with the strange and different practices these people cherished. In Tildens, he would arrive at the tiny wooden one-room church to find 10 or 12 men standing around their buggies, talking about ranching and rustlers and farmers and thieves. Inside, the women and children would be sitting on crude wooden benches on the right side of the room. At 11:00 a.m., the people would begin singing, by "lining." There were no hymn books, so the song leader would first sing a phrase alone and then the women would sing the phrase back, and so on. When the music was finished, the men would file in and sit on the opposite side of the room. While most real traveling preachers—both Methodist and Baptist— found these local customs to be, at times, irritating, Cole didn't pay any attention to them. He would come in, read from his scruffy little Bible, say a few words, and be on his way. However, the reason Cole's preaching career lasted as long as it did was what his parishioners viewed as his innate and God-given talent to heal people in all kinds of ways.

Cole truly was a wanderer during this time. He never knew where he would sleep and didn't much care. Wherever he happened to be at suppertime was where he generally spent the night. And when that opportunity didn't happen to present itself, he camped out under the great live oaks.

One Tuesday afternoon, Cole stopped at the ranch belonging to Major Tom McKnight. As he pulled up to the low, rambling clapboard house, Tom's younger boy, George, came running out to meet him. "Preacher, Daddy's hurt," the boy yelled, as he practically dragged Cole off his horse and into the house. George, in a frantic stutter, quickly told Cole that his dad had been knocked off his horse while riding through the swamp a mile or two from the house. His foot had caught in the stirrup, and he was dragged a distance before he finally worked it free. He lay on the ground for an hour before his boys found him. Their mother was away, and the two boys had struggled to drag their father into the house.

Cole looked at the man lying in his bed. The bedclothes were soaked with mud and blood. The older son, who had gone to find the doctor, soon appeared in the room, looking scared. "I can't find him nowhere!" the boy cried.

Cole asked the boys to bring warm water. With his bowie knife, Cole cut Tom's clothes from his body. When the boys returned with water from the stove, they stood staring at their naked father and the large, gaping wound down the side of his thigh. Cole took the pot of tepid water and slowly poured it into the wound. The water soaked the bed linens and ran down to the floor. After flushing the wound several times, Cole said, "Tom, your boys and I are gonna clean you up." Tom looked up in disbelief but said nothing.

The boys brought soap and more water, and Cole proceeded to clean Tom's body from top to bottom. He asked the boys to help, but they just stared at the man giving their father a bath. Cole gently washed away mud and debris, finding no other serious injuries, but the long, gaping wound on Tom's left side was oozing blood. "Go fetch your mother's sewing basket," he instructed George.

After a small struggle threading the needle, Cole proceeded to sew up Tom's wound. When he was finished, Cole and the boys moved Tom to the other bed in the room. Once Tom was dressed in a clean nightshirt and asleep in the clean bed, Cole said to the boys, "You better gather up those dirty bed clothes and boil them before your mom comes home, or she'll kill all of us."

Cole stayed until the doctor arrived the next day. Shaking his head at Cole's unorthodox ways, the doctor begrudgingly admitted that he probably had saved Tom's life.

CHAPTER SEVENTEEN

Early Feminism

• • •

D uring the short time Cole was a Methodist preacher, he managed to stay out of trouble with women. The truth was Cole respected women. His mother had been an intelligent, strong, loving woman. He had known more cracker women like her, who could stand up to any man, and he developed a special kind of respect for the church-going wives he encountered on the circuit. Even though they lived miles from each other, the women were instrumental in starting churches and then holding them together.

The Florida frontier was a lonely place and many women suffered severe depression. Some went back up north and others even killed themselves. But Cole could see that religion and Christian support really did sustain some of them through the crises of going broke, babies dying, and husbands being absent or mistreating them. They would come together regularly to quilt and gossip and help each other with sick kids. He noticed that the women who made the effort and found the time and energy to look out for those in need seemed to be much happier than the ones who were isolated.

Cole's perception of women differed from that of most of the cattlemen in the interior wilderness in the late 1800s. It was a man's world, and in this country, most men didn't have the time or inclination to treat women well. Cole sometimes wondered why the women put up with it, since they worked as hard as the men did. He also knew that many of the men were plain mean—even some of the Methodists.

One day, when Cole was camping out by Starke Lake in the St. Johns River valley, two men he knew from the Mt. Pisgah Church rode up.

"Glad we found ya, Reverend," one of the men called out. Cole always wanted to look over his shoulder to see who people were talking to when they used that title. It wasn't just because he felt like a fraud. He knew he was a fraud.

The two men got off their horses and proceeded to tell Cole something that seemed incredulous, although he didn't doubt for a minute that it was true. They were heading into town when they heard a woman yelling her head off. As they rode toward the sound, they came to a clearing where they saw a two-wheeled wagon. On the far side of the wagon, they found the woman. Her hands and feet were tied, and one end of the rope was looped up over the frame of the wagon and tied securely on the other side. There was a bucket of water beside the woman so that, with a serious struggle, she could get a drink. The younger of the men began to untie her when she said, "My man, Mr. Hobie, done this to me." The older man then raised his hand to motion the younger man to stop.

"Why'd he do this, Miz Hobie?"

"We was comin' back from gettin' supplies in Sanford. Mr. Hobie said he was tired of me naggin him. I just wanted to stay in town a little bit longer to talk with my women friends. But he was mad and stopped the wagon, dragged me out, and tied me up. Said he was goin' home without me, and he'd be back in the mornin' to get me and the supplies." The older man thought a minute and said, "Sorry, ma'am. We can't interfere with a man punishin' his wife." And they left her tied up and sitting in the dirt next to the wagon wheel, sobbing.

When they were a mile or so down the dirt road, which was really nothing more than a path cut through the woods, the older man began thinking about nightfall and what might happen to the woman. She would be at the mercy of the animals. And October nights could get cold. While he was still thinking, they stumbled onto Cole's campsite.

Cole listened to the story. He didn't say a word, but they were familiar with the strange preacher's silences.

Cole didn't speak because the men's refusal to help the woman enraged him. What he really wanted to do was to leave the two of them tied to the great live oak he was camping under. As they spoke, Cole broke up camp, packed his belongings, and saddled his horse. He tipped his hat and headed east. The men knew where he was going.

Cole found the woman singing hymns, as he rode up. When she saw him, she began to cry, saying, "Preacher am I glad to see you!" As he untied her he asked, "Are you hurt?"

"I don't think so. Just tired, hungry, and scar't."

While the woman washed her face, Cole cut up some oranges he found in the wagon and began to set up camp.

"Ain't we goin' home, preacher?"

"No, I don't think Mr. Hobie means to leave you here overnight. I think he'll be back soon. Let's wait a spell."

The woman walked around a bit and rubbed her arms while Cole started a fire and began to make coffee. After she got supplies from the wagon, they sat on the ground and ate.

About an hour later, Mr. Hobie came riding up. He brought the two cracker horses with him to hitch to the wagon. He eyes Cole and the woman sitting under the tree, drinking coffee.

"Preacher, you got no right comin' between a man and his wife." Cole stood up and as soon as the man got off his horse, he hit him in the face with his fist. The man staggered back and fell to the ground unconscious. Cole and the woman poured water on Mr. Hobie. As soon as he began to come to, Mrs. Hobie tore off a strip of her petticoat and began dabbing at her husband's bleeding nose. At the same time, she began screaming at Cole, "Preacher, there was no cause to hit him!"

Cole gathered up his things, and without another word, went on his way. He knew that the moment his fist hit Mr. Hobie's face, his career as a Methodist preacher was over. That night he found a card game, got drunk, and lost all of his money.

CHAPTER EIGHTEEN

THE MAKING OF A WRITER
• • •

A young Catherine Richardson was standing on the deck of the Amsterdam, feeling at once defeated and elated. She was beginning her voyage home to Boston from the English countryside where she had been visiting for several months. She had missed her father and was excited at the thought of seeing him, but knew he would be sorely disappointed that, at 26, she was still unmarried. For him, that had been the sole mission for Catherine's trip. And she knew it.

John Richardson was a professor at Boston College. He was a widower and Catherine was his only child. He had hoped that her time in England would help Catherine settle down and learn to accept the realities of life for women in the 19th century. Life was passing her by. He was sure of it. Just the week before, he had read the popular saying in a campus magazine, *What possible use does a woman over 40 have on this earth?* And now Catherine would return home, still unmarried and with no prospects.

It wasn't that Catherine didn't have suitors. She did. She was just never particularly interested in any of them.

After graduation from Rutland College, Catherine had taught for several years at the prestigious Hartsfield School, but as a gifted writer, her passion was discovering life's adventures and writing about them.

Getting the kinds of stories Catherine wrote published was impossible, given they were written by an old maid schoolteacher. So, Professor Richardson, who functioned as her agent, and his daughter shared a secret known only to them. The popular adventure stories by J. T. Scott that appeared from time to time in several magazines around the country were written by Catherine, who had had a vivid fantasy life since she was a little girl.

When her mother was sent to a tuberculosis sanitarium, Catherine was six years old. Unable to cope with a little girl alone, her father sent her to an Episcopal boarding school in the city of Boston. Although she came home on the weekends, life was hard because he spent Sundays with Catherine's mother at the sanitarium.

Only allowed to visit her mother once a month, the young girl spent most of her weekends with a series of nannies. And gradually, Catherine's mother faded into a virtual stranger who showed little interest in the child. The Episcopal school emphasized a well-balanced life for young ladies. The students were to strive to be healthy physically, mentally, and spiritually. To that end, Catherine spent one hour each day in silent "prayer" and 10 hours each night in bed. This was the beginning of her lifelong challenge with insomnia.

Over the years she compensated for the forced idleness by assembling complicated and (to her) intriguing stories in her mind. As for her physical health, she dealt with the massive amount of food placed on her plate at mealtimes the same way all the girls did—by finding exotic places to hide it. Many years later, when she and her father visited the school, he and the head mistress were commenting on how beautifully the old, heavy drapes in the dining room had held up over the years. Catherine then proceeded to show them the bulky, wide hems where generations of little girls had hidden beans, peas, and other assorted vegetables that subsequently had hardened and weighed down the massive drapes, rendering them wrinkle free.

CHAPTER NINETEEN

A Different Kind of Woman
• • •

John Richardson had made arrangements with mutual friends for Catherine to be the houseguest of the McBride's, a couple in their 60s, for the three months she would be in England. Although the time with her hosts was interesting and fun and she attended all kinds of social gatherings, she soon learned how to wiggle out of invitations designed to get her matched up with a potential suitor. Howard and his wife, Camellia, had one brief discussion regarding Catherine's inability to find romantic love with a man, but never spoke of it again. She spent much of her time reading and writing.

To Howard and Camellia's consternation, Catherine persisted in striking up involved personal conversations with the servants. The McBrides didn't know what to make of this unpredictable American woman, but they did like her.

It was not that Catherine found men unattractive; it was just that her conversational style and demeanor were straightforward and democratic in nature, and she had a complete inability to flirt. This was, to her father's grave concern, a decided drawback in upper-class society in the British Isles as well as in Boston.

Howard McBride was, of all things, originally from Texas. After becoming rich in the oil fields, he had severed all ties with his wife of 20 years whom he rarely had seen. He then traveled to England and promptly fell in love with a proper Englishwoman from Bath. After they married and settled into a quiet British life, it soon became evident that Howard was not well suited for sedate living. Even though he loved the woman and she was everything he could hope for in a wife, the oilfields of Texas were calling him home.

When Catherine arrived, McBride was in a crisis, of sorts. He understood that—if he got to the point that he no longer could resist returning to Texas—his wife would refuse to go with him. So when the high-spirited houseguest expressed an interest in riding lessons, McBride agreed to be her instructor—reasoning that the assignment might keep him in England a while longer. And although Catherine did not take her father's advice to pursue a husband while on her trip to England, she did take horseback riding lessons.

The Texan tried to insist that she use an English saddle, but she finally wore him down and eventually, used a western saddle exclusively. Catherine had ridden before but under McBride's tutelage, she quickly became somewhat of an expert equestrian. Catherine rode like a man, as she explored the countryside. She often dressed like one too, and some of McBride's neighbors thought she was a young boy, as the horse she rode galloped through the surrounding woods.

In the evenings, Howard entertained Camellia and Catherine with tall stories of what it was like to constantly find new adventure in the Southwestern United States. Catherine wondered whether that might be a place for her–someone who was not like other women. Otherwise, the only place she really belonged appeared to be in the stories she wrote.

The day eventually came when Catherine would sail home to face her father's disappointment, when he would learn that his investment in finding her a husband had failed.

CHAPTER TWENTY

COULD IT BE THE WATER?

• • •

The second day at sea, Catherine met Sam Hamilton. She went to high tea at 4:00 p.m., wearing her only dress that was appropriate for such things. As she entered the area, she saw him standing alone looking at the paintings of great sailing ships on the walls surrounding the room. A ship's officer noticed Catherine staring at the lone man and immediately escorted her over to him and introduced the two. When Catherine later looked back on that moment, she couldn't exactly say she had liked Samuel Hamilton. There was an aloofness about him that bordered on antisocial behavior, which she correctly guessed to be a mask for loneliness. But from that first glimpse of him, Catherine knew her life would never be the same again. She was in love with him, and she knew he would become her husband.

Very soon after they were introduced, Sam asked, "Would you care to have dinner with me this evening?"

"I'm not sure," Catherine replied, while at the same time trying to think of a way to get out of her previous shipboard dinner obligations.

91

But Sam, being as straightforward as Catherine, finally said, "Well, do you or don't you want to have dinner with me?" She did, and the rest, as they say, is history.

Professor John Richardson was overwhelmed with pleasure when he received the news that his daughter had fallen in love and wanted to be married as soon as the proper arrangements could be made. When he met Samuel Hamilton, he found him to be a bit strange and seemingly unsure of himself, but Sam's background and wealth outweighed Professor Hamilton's fears about his eccentricities.

Sam and Catherine were married at the Episcopal Church on February 22, 1882. Catherine was 27 years old. Her family and friends thought she was fortunate, indeed, to have found a suitable husband at this advanced age.

But there was trouble right away. Neither Catherine nor Sam was contented. Although they loved each other, they struggled with a longing that could not be fully explained or held at bay. And of course, Catherine's independent spirit that initially had attracted Sam soon began to get on his nerves. It seemed that every decision was a challenge. They both wanted to explore new territory. Catherine thought that going back to Europe where they could experience the intellectual community and she could write would help both of them. Sam was an outdoorsman and felt stifled in the city. He wanted to go west. There was still a frontier and new vistas were opening all the time. Catherine sometimes felt that marrying a man just because you loved him might be a recipe for misery.

The trouble was that Catherine realized she was not as adventurous as she projected herself or even longed to be. One of the reasons Sam was so attractive to her was that she knew he would push her to go places she had never been. But, partly because of Howard McBride's wild stories, the western frontier just felt too risky for her to seriously consider.

Four months after the wedding, Professor Richardson threw a grand party for the newlyweds. It had taken this long to get things organized. After Catherine's mother died, entertaining had always been a challenge for him. And as Catherine grew older, he had depended a great deal on her to take on this responsibility. But he did not want her to help this time, as it was a gift to her.

The house and everything in it sparkled. Catherine wore a white lace dress, which was quite a departure from her usual tailored attire. She and Sam mingled with the crowd and enjoyed the elaborate food being served both in the dining room and on the wide porch surrounding the entire Victorian house.

Professor Richardson introduced Sam and Catherine to a former student and friend of his named John Chandler. Mr. Chandler had just returned from several months in Florida, and Catherine was eager to hear what it was really like there. She had imagined only alligators and swamps, but as the rugged, suntanned rancher talked, Catherine and Sam realized that Chandler was describing another frontier–one with all the excitement of the west. Florida was idyllic, where fortunes were being made amidst cattle ranches, Indians, and rustlers. And the new railroad coming through would bring civilization to this primitive paradise.

The next day, without too much trouble really, Sam talked Catherine into moving to Florida. They would plan to stay for three years to see if they could make it as ranchers. Catherine thought she could stand anything for that long and it would give her new things to write about.

She never could have imagined what was in store down the road ahead in her future.

CHAPTER TWENTY-ONE

WOMAN IN BLACK

• • •

The one-horse surrey clipped along the dirt road leading to the small town of Oconee in North Orange County. Catherine was alone, pulling the reins of the small horse. At only four hands high, the "cracker' horse was common in Florida. The horse was small, but strong enough to do the work of any normal size horse and the cracker horse adapted easily to the Florida heat. Proper widow's wear replaced the strange, strong, and seductive attire of the day before, and Catherine was wearing a black dress that covered her entire body and a large black hat.

She pulled up in front of the bank five minutes before the appointed time for her meeting with the bank president, Robert Laundry, and Robert Barton.

Once inside the small wooden building, Catherine was escorted by the bank clerk to an enclosed office, where they were waiting for her. Although almost no conversation took place, Robert Barton did express surprise that her "friend" was not with her. She ignored the comment. The papers were signed and Barton handed over the agreed-upon $20,000 in cash to Catherine in a large carpetbag. If the men were wondering about the naiveté of a woman traveling back to her home with a fortune in cash, they did not show it. Neither did the bank president suggest she deposit the money back into the bank. She left the office without a handshake, knowing they were all aware that Robert Barton was responsible for the murder of her husband. She also knew they had no intention of letting her leave the area with their $20,000.

CHAPTER TWENTY-TWO

A FORK IN THE ROAD

• • •

A bout four miles out of town on the way back to the Hamilton Ranch, there was a fork in the road. Veering right would lead to the Hamilton's closest neighbor—the Wilsons. Chester Wilson was off with his ranch hands driving cattle, and his wife, Theda, and the girls were visiting Theda's family in Georgia. The ranch was deserted. Instead of heading left at the fork, toward home, Catherine veered right and traveled the two miles down the old dirt path that led to the Wilson's.

She pulled the buggy all the way into the open barn. Cole was waiting there for her with fresh horses. They quickly dissembled the buggy and pushed it into a stall. They sent the cracker horse that had pulled the buggy into the holding pen. Catherine transferred the money from her carpetbag to the saddlebags Cole had ready for her. Then she pulled a full set of clothing—britches, boots, shirt, and jacket out from under the buggy's covering. Seeming to be unmindful of Cole, she pulled off the black dress, revealing a full set of long woolen underwear—obviously sized for a young boy.

 Wool undergarments and unshrinkable flannels were the preferred clothing choices for males in Florida.

Catherine quickly slipped on the set of clothes. When she lifted off her black hat, Cole stared. Her long auburn hair was gone. She had the close-cropped bad haircut of a young boy. She took the petticoat that she had removed with the dress and rubbed her face hard to remove the makeup she had applied early that morning. Cole could not believe the transformation. This beautiful woman now looked like a skinny, teenage boy.

Catherine gathered up the dress, hat, petticoat, and shoes and threw them onto a huge manure pile in the corner. Then she found a pitchfork and flipped the pile, making sure to completely cover the clothes. Next, she and Cole lifted a small trunk from the buggy. They found shovels, and, in a corner of the barn, they dug a hole, buried the old trunk, and covered the site with hay. The trunk contained everything remaining of her life in Florida because, before leaving the ranch that morning, she and Cole had burned her house down to the ground.

CHAPTER TWENTY-THREE

ON THE RUN

• • •

Their work on the Wilson Ranch took about half an hour. When they finished, they climbed onto fresh horses, rode to the stream, and then went upstream for about two miles. After crossing the stream at a narrow spot, they started their descent into the swamp.

Cole knew every trail, where the ranch lands began and ended, and where the Indians camped. He also knew where rustlers and other outlaws were likely to be. All of this provided Catherine with a sense of security that seemed somewhat strange to her, under the circumstances.

They stayed off the main trails and picked their way through the forests. They rode close to the river, as the bright sun etched the images of the tall pines in the water. And they were careful to stay clear of the thick mud, muck, and quicksand that tended to swallow up intruders deep in the woods. To her surprise, Catherine felt alive for the first time since that awful day.

In the winter, Florida's waters were clear as glass. But summer's sunshine and heat brought thick weeds and undergrowth that effectively hid the alligators and other dangerous creatures. For this reason, most people didn't travel alongside the state's rivers in the summertime.

They stopped along the Little Wekiva in a cove where Cole knew it was unlikely they'd be seen, even on the slight chance that another human being might be in the area. While they were planning the trip, Catherine had informed Cole that she knew most everything about horses but nothing about camping. So Catherine bedded the horses while Cole started a fire.

It was almost dark when Cole put beans, grits, and bacon on a tin plate and handed it to her. She handed back the bacon. After they ate, he took the bedrolls she had removed from the horses and placed them head-to-head under the towering oaks and scrub palms. Catherine took the money-filled saddlebag and put it at the top of her bedroll to use as a pillow and lay down. She took the gun that Sam had bought in Orlando—the one she'd begged him to get rid of because she feared what it represented—and laid it across her chest.

"Put that gun away," Cole said. "You're gonna get us both killed or more likely you're gonna shoot me by mistake."

"If I shoot you, it won't be by mistake," Catherine replied, as she closed her eyes.

But Catherine had no fear of Cole hurting her. She remembered the folklore that had been whispered around about Cole. She'd heard stories from people at small Methodist gatherings, townspeople who had hired him as the temporary sheriff, and those who had benefited from his considerable medicinal talents. She wondered what Cole would think if he knew that even she, herself, had stories about him.

A year or so after moving to Florida—and long before ever personally meeting Cole—Catherine had written a letter to her father.

Dear Father,

The stories we heard about Florida being a wild frontier are all true. We have settled in on our land and Sam is becoming quite a rancher. But we are always and ever alert for rustlers, wild animals, swindlers, bad weather, sick cattle, and the complications and dangers involved with the railroad coming through.

Father, I have written a story about a character I've heard about from time to time. He is as much a cowboy legend as anyone we've heard about out west. His name is Coleman Wills. Please query our publishers about accepting an adventure story titled, "A Florida Cowboy."

Your faithful daughter,

Catherine

Nine weeks later Catherine received this reply.

My Dear Catherine,

Our publishers are not interested in an adventure story from Florida. They believe the only people settling there are invalids and others who cannot tolerate the cold weather and hard work of the north. I will be appreciative when you and Samuel get this ranching experience out of your systems and come back to Boston, where you belong.

Yours,

Father

Around midnight, Cole woke up with a start. Catherine was sobbing and muttering to herself. She was sitting upright with the gun by her side. He crawled over from his bedroll and put his hands firmly on her upper arms.

"Wake up, you're not there. You're here. You're safe."

She was rigid. She stared at Cole and tried to bring her mind back to the present.

"I'm sorry," was all she finally said, as she lay back down. Cole went back to his bedroll to wait for sunrise and set out again.

Catherine lay on the ground, looking at the stars. She thought about her life with Sam. She thought about the many things that had happened from the minute they arrived in Florida to the moment Sam drew his last breath. Were those "in between" things completely unrelated to Sam's death? Were they simply coincidental? Looking back from the vantage point of what she'd seen and been through—and where she lay now—she didn't think so.

Shortly after their arrival in Central Florida, there had been a special mayoral election in the tiny town of Oconee. Sam wasn't sure whether he was eligible to vote, but he had voted in every election since he became of age and wanted to find out. The circuit judge, who just happened to be in the office that day, told Sam that, although he legally could vote, he advised against it. He reasoned that Sam had only been there a short time and didn't know how things worked. Sam thought that was nonsense.

The two candidates had a lot in common, but one—Costello Selby—was a well-known land grabber with close ties to Robert Barton. The main reason Sam voted against Selby, though, was that he was an avowed racist and demonstrated it every time he had the chance. Voting was held in the schoolhouse. There was not much secrecy since you had to mark your choice on a piece of paper and hand it to the man in charge. Costello Selby won by a landslide. The next day, the votes were posted in the saloon window: Thirty-seven for Selby; one for Selby's opponent. There was no doubt in anybody's mind who had cast the lone ballet against the winner.

CHAPTER TWENTY-FOUR

THE PACT

• • •

Before leaving the Hamilton Ranch, Catherine and Cole had agreed that he would help her sell the ranch and then take her to Cassadaga, in exchange for 10 percent of the money from the sale of the ranch. Not even a real town, Cassadaga was a place just north of the prestigious town of Enterprise that Sam had referred to as a gathering place for misfits. Despite gossip that "crazy things" went on there, the place was full of fairly normal, albeit wounded people, who just wanted to be left alone.

Founded by George Colby, Cassadaga started as a place for spiritualists to gather and explore the supernatural. Colby, however, credited it to an Indian guide named Seneca who, during a séance in Lake Mills, Iowa, instructed Colby to establish a spiritualist community in the south. After following instructions from Seneca, Colby arrived at a place near Orange City, called Blue Springs Landing. Seneca later guided him through the pathless wilds to an area that had been shown to him during the séance. In 1875, Colby named the camp Cassadaga, after a spiritualist community on the outskirts of Lily Dale, New York. Eventually it became known as a place of peace

and sanctuary for people longing for healing. But, in addition to
the spirit seekers, there were old prostitutes, burned-out lawmen,
other misfits, and people who couldn't get over a serious loss in
their lives. Some would stay a while, and others would remain
longer in this quiet place, where people looked out for each other.

Catherine had heard the stories about Cassadaga and was
fascinated. She had tried to get Sam to take her there. She wanted
to talk to the people and find out what had driven them to this
sanctuary. She even had studied the Bible to find the origin of that
word, *sanctuary*, and she discovered that it was "a dwelling place
for God," where people could be safe. And she knew from studying
history that, in the early churches, if people in trouble could find
their way to the sanctuary of the church, they would not be turned
over to the authorities. Likewise, Catherine knew that the Bible
plainly said not to associate with spiritualists. But this did not
dissuade her in the least because, as a writer, she was curious and
wanted to investigate and learn more. Sam, however, would not
hear of it.

Now, while enduring the intolerable loss and pain of Sam's death,
she wanted to go somewhere safe, so she could gain strength and
figure out what to do next. Of course, she *thought* she knew what
to do. And that was to go back to Oconee and kill the men who
had destroyed her life. It was an insane idea, but, at the moment, it
was the only thing that kept her moving. What she knew for sure,
though, was that she needed sanctuary.

Their first night on the trail, after a particularly disturbing
and violent afternoon, she helped Cole clean his wounds and

encouraged him to drink from the small bottle of "home brew" he carried and gave to those in serious physical pain. After he was asleep, she settled in to write in her journal about the strange, frightening day. She had to admit to herself that, even though Cole was almost always in the right, sometimes he dealt with problems in exceedingly self-destructive ways.

CHAPTER TWENTY-FIVE

UNJUST

• • •

We camped in a bog next to a majestic bald cypress. It was early afternoon, and we were indulging ourselves with a nap after lunch. Cole heard the sounds of horse and wagon long before I did. We ran about a quarter of a mile and climbed up the side of a hill to take a look. Cole wasn't particularly concerned because we were well hidden and he was, above all things, a master in the art of observation.

After a while, we saw the wagon coming up the sun-drenched trail. A black preacher drove the team. Cole knew this, and explained, "Nobody but preachers wear black suits in the middle of a weekday afternoon."

Two little boys* were in the back of the wagon. Even I could see they were twins. They looked exactly alike. Just as we were about to scramble back down the hill, Cole heard other horses. Momentarily, three riders galloped up to the wagon with guns drawn, and the preacher quickly pulled in the reins. I couldn't hear everything they said but the men were laughing as they got down off their horses so I decided it couldn't be too bad. Pretty soon, the preacher climbed *down from the wagon, as the little boys, huddled in the back, wide eyed. Then I heard one of the riders shout, "Dance, nigger!" and they began to fire shots at the man's feet. As the dignified looking black man in the black suit began to shuffle his feet, I thought it was just about the saddest thing I've ever seen. Tears welled in my eyes as I crouched in the weeds.*

I don't know why I was not aware that Cole had left my side, but suddenly, he bounded out of the woods. He grabbed one of the gunmen around the ankles causing him to fall hard to the ground. The other two men looked startled, but they were on top of Cole, pummeling him with their fists. When they were finished, they got on their horses and rode off. I ran down the hill and when I reached Cole, the preacher was hovering over him, wiping his blood-filled mouth. Looking terrified, the little boys never left the wagon. After a while, Cole revived enough to insist that the preacher go along on his journey. I helped him back to the camp and tried my best to clean him up and get him to talk to me. I was furious and rambled on about what a stupid thing he had done, but he wouldn't say a word.

*In years to follow, the twins would cross Catherine's path, again and again. Both of the boys would grow up to follow the example their father had set and become United Methodist ministers.

CHAPTER TWENTY-SIX

FATIGUE

• • •

Catherine and Cole rode the next morning until the sun was almost directly overhead. Cole acted as if nothing unusual had happened the day before, but neither he nor Catherine had an appetite, Catherine experienced an increasing number of other symptoms that made her suspect something might be very wrong.

They continued to stay in the wooded and swampy areas, as they were sure that Robert Barton and his men were looking for them. They planned to camp in the deep woods for a few days, knowing that Barton would be expecting them to leave Central Florida.

But the afternoon the following day, Catherine was too tired to stay in the saddle. They stopped in a small clearing beside a stream, and she lay down on a blanket of pine needles without even bothering to put down her bedroll. While Cole scouted around on foot, Catherine tried to stay awake and to focus on good thoughts. The breeze reminded her of the trip she and Sam had made to the ocean. He had never let her live it down.

CHAPTER TWENTY-SEVEN

SAND, SURF, & SALT

• • •

Catherine knew that Florida had more than 1,350 miles of coastline. She always thought that, on the map, it looked like a huge thumb dipping into the Atlantic Ocean. Growing up in Boston, she was familiar with the ocean, but it would never occur to a proper Bostonian to come into personal contact with it. One day, when Catherine was a child and they were seeing friends off at the pier, she thought of jumping right into the murky water, but her father's firm grip stopped her.

Years later, while traveling to and from England, she loved the experience of standing on deck, as the waves pounded the sides of the ship. At that point, thoughts of being in the water came only in conjunction with something going terribly wrong. After moving to Florida, though, she heard stories of the wonders of the state's beaches. Tales of white sand, fascinating seashells, cool breezes, breathtaking sun rises on the East Coast, and magnificent sunsets on the peninsula's West Coast all made her long for this adventure. She did not want to leave Florida without the experience of swimming in the salty ocean. After she badgered Sam for months, he relented, knowing that she was like water dripping on a rock in her determination to get what she wanted.

They set out one day in early September. They rode to Orlando and spent the night in a boarding house on Church Street. At dawn the next morning, they boarded a stagecoach for Titusville.

Under ideal travel conditions, a coach driven by a fresh team of horses could travel nine miles per hour, so a 50-mile trip, like one from Orlando to Titusville, could be made in one day. However, driving conditions were rarely ideal. With bad roads and often drunk drivers at the reins, passengers could expect the coach to turn over at least once on a trip. Men would be warned not to grease their hair before a coach ride because it would attract great quantities of dirt and sand. They also were warned to ride with their backs to the horses, which made some people "seasick." The nausea, though, would wear off on long trips, and passengers in those seats would get more rest and endure fewer bumps and jars, than those in any other seat.

They did make the trip in one day, but only because they made a very short stop at Fort Christmas for fresh horses and twilight did not come until almost 9:00 p.m. Luck was with them, and they had no major misadventures on the trip. Although about 15 miles from Titusville the road did become so rough that it was almost impassable, so they and the other passengers had to climb out and walk about a quarter of a mile behind the coach as it jostled over the bumpy terrain.

That night they stayed in Titusville with an old friend from Boston, Harold Tyson. Sam had relented about the trip because Harold had agreed to make all of the arrangements to get them to the beach, where they would camp for two nights. For many weeks prior to the trip, Sam and Harold had corresponded the way most people did, by postcards.

The following morning, Harold, Catherine, and Sam crossed the intercoastal waterway, which ran all the way down the east coast of the United States. Harold had made arrangement for them to cross in a boat at a point called the Banana River.

From the far shore, Catherine and Sam piled their belongings and camping equipment Harold had for them into a conestoga wagon. Then, they drove several miles on a trail through the thickest Florida jungle Catherine had ever seen. Just as she was thinking about calling it quits, apologizing to Sam, and suggesting they turn around to go back home, they came to a clearing.

Overwhelmed by the massive beauty before them, they just sat in the wagon for a few minutes and took in the mind-boggling scene. It was all horizontal. The first thing Catherine thought about was the "three-tiered universe" theory she used to discuss with her students. Many of their grandparents, even the highly educated ones, still harbored a belief that the universe consisted of three horizontal entities: earth, sky, and heaven. As far as Catherine, Sam, and Harold could see in either direction–and they could see for miles and miles–there was a wide horizontal ribbon of sand that bordered the ocean. It was the most beautiful, powerful, and frightening sight Catherine could ever remember having seen. And then there was a skyline that never ceased. Before seeing all of this, Catherine had believed that Florida's monotonously flat surface showed the biggest sky imaginable. This ocean view, however, topped anything she ever could have dreamed of.

Sam loved riddles and Catherine remembered the day he teasingly asked her how far she could see, and she answered, "I don't know, maybe five miles on a clear day."

He laughed and said, "You can see thousands of miles away. You can see the sun!"

After helping unload the camping equipment and instructing them where to set up camp, Harold left Sam and Catherine to their camping adventure. They had agreed to camp for two days, but as Harold was pulling away in the wagon, he said, "I'll check on you tomorrow afternoon."

After they set up camp in the woods a few feet from the beach, Catherine changed into the swimming suit she had bought before leaving Boston. Black, with sleeves extending to the wrists and legs ending at the ankles, the suit had white ruffles covering the entire bodice and a short overlaying skirt with rows of pleats.

Catherine walked the 20 or so yards from the campsite to the water's edge. The sand was warm and gave her feet a tingly massage. She dipped a toe into the cold water and then slowly treaded out a few feet. She wondered why she had been frightened, and as the little waves gingerly lapped at her calves, she silently questioned what Harold had been talking about when he warned them to be careful if they went into the water.

Most people were aware of the tides but found it hard to believe that the ocean could be 50 yards out at low tide and yet completely lap up a campsite at high tide. As Catherine faced the shore, looking for Sam, she heard a roar behind her back. Before she could look around, a wave had lifted her off her feet. As she struggled to right herself, another wave washed over her, pulling her out further with it. She was terrified as she struggled for air. Where was she? She was disoriented. Salt water was rushing through her sinus cavities as she tumbled to and fro. She wondered, "Is this the way it will end? Drowning in the Atlantic Ocean without a human being in sight?"

Then she finally found her footing. And when the waves receded, she realized she was standing in water that barely came to her knees. She began laughing out loud and started to move toward shore just as she saw the next wave coming. But it was hard going because every little pocket of the swimming suit, every little seam and ruffle was filled with sand. She made her way back to the campsite where Sam was preparing a fishing line. She grabbed his knife and began cutting at the suit. With the skirt and all the ruffles cut away, all that remained on Catherine's body was the form-fitting tank. Sam laughed and said, "Don't run into Mrs. Wilson on your way back to the water."

Catherine spent the rest of the day swimming, playing, and looking for shells. She soon learned how to relax and let the waves carry her back to shore. She wondered why people of means didn't spend all of their time at the ocean.

That evening her skin began to itch. There wasn't enough drinking water for her to use for a freshwater bath. She had visible patches of salt on her red and burning body. After a bad night's sleep outdoors under the mosquito netting and after Sam had fixed them a breakfast of fresh ocean perch, she walked for a time on the beach looking for shells.

On the way back, she saw something glistening in the sun. It was some kind of sea creature washed up on the shore. It looked like a beautiful blue, translucent ball with long blue tentacles trailing from it. Catherine wanted to push it back into the water. She found a stick and tried to push it into a receding wave, but it wouldn't budge. Finally, she reached down with her hand to grab one of the tentacles and, brushing her arm against the others; she felt a sharp, excruciating pain. Welts immediately appeared on her arm. She ran back to Sam. He poured water on the welts, but there was very little relief. Sam said, "I've read about something that will stop the pain but you're not going to like the idea." "I'll try anything," she said as she dug her fingernails into her palm.

When Harold arrived that afternoon to check on them, they were packed up and ready for the trip home. That evening, Catherine had a long bath in the kitchen tub at Harold's log house in Titusville. It was the best, most soothing bath she ever had taken. She couldn't imagine ever telling anyone about what Sam had done to quiet the pain in her arm from the sea creature and the itch of her skin from the salt water. However, she knew that someday she definitely would write a story about the medicinal powers of urine.

CHAPTER TWENTY-EIGHT

A Skinny Boy

• • •

C atherine had fallen asleep for an hour or so while Cole planned where they would go next and then they climbed back on their horses and rode. Her whole body felt like it was on fire, so she wasn't too unhappy when they came out of the pine forest and she saw the sketchiness of a town a few miles ahead of them.

"I figure you need some rest," Cole said.

She should have been upset. This was not part of their deal. And it was dangerous. She suspected, though, that Cole was heading for this town for his own purposes as well as hers.

The town of Sanford was known as Mellonville, before Henry Sanford arrived in the late 1800s. The original name was given to the town when, in 1837, the Seminole Indians raided the nearby military staging area. The raid was not successful, but they did manage to kill Capt. Charles Mellon.

In 1879, General Henry Sanford laid out the town of Sanford near Mellonville on the south side of the St. Johns River. Cattle ranching was still king in the area, but there were constant battles between ranchers on one side and farmers and railroad barons on the other. General Sanford's vision was to stimulate citrus growing and other agricultural pursuits. Rail lines were beginning to connect the more flourishing towns and he had the foresight to know that this eventually would change Florida forever, in spite the ranchers' resistance.

As Catherine and Cole rode down the middle of the dirt road that led to the town, they looked every bit like a cowboy and a kid. The two had decided that Cole would refer to Catherine as "Jack."
At the Sanford Hotel and Saloon, Cole asked for the room with the little room behind it. It was the only room in the hotel with an adjacent room. The only entrance to the small room was through the larger room. After registering, they walked the horses the short distance to the livery.

John Toms had been the stable hand at the Mellonville Livery for 18 years. Jack took the horses, and as she was turning the reins over to the old man, he said, "Where you comin' from?"

Jack lowered her head and grunted out an answer as she circled the horses.

"You kin to Cole?" This question startled her, partly because this man knew Cole and partly because it was her first time to have to explain their relationship.

"Nephew," Jack answered.

"What? I can't hear you, boy."

Jack took a breath and said,

"Him and my momma was brother and sister."

She said this more confidently because she realized he had called her "boy."

Cole had been standing in the corner listening to the conversation. He left the stable with the skinny boy and went back to the hotel, carrying the saddlebag and other gear. The two sat at a back table and had supper. Then Jack went to the little room in back, took off her clothes, washed herself as best she could, using the bowl and pitcher on the table, got back into the long johns, and went to bed. She didn't wake up until the next day.

CHAPTER TWENTY-NINE

THE BANK TRANSACTION

• • •

As Jack's eyes came into focus, she realized she had slept about 14 hours. She dressed and then peeked into the other room. Cole wasn't there. The room was exactly as it had been when the hotel clerk had shown it to them the day before. She went back to her room and hid the saddlebag by stuffing it underneath the ornate old wardrobe. Then she went to find Cole. It wasn't hard. He was in the back of the saloon playing poker. It was obvious from just looking at him that he'd spent the night there. She walked into the room and stood behind his chair, but he ignored her. She turned around and walked out.

She went back to the little diner a few doors down where they'd had a meal the night before. A woman came over and said, "Hey, kid, what'll you have?"

Jack was again hesitant about speaking but lowered her voice and gave the woman her breakfast order without making eye contact.

The woman said, "You sure are a shy one. You got any money, kid?"

"Yeah, Cole gave me money."

That was all it took. The woman walked away and returned in a few minutes with the eggs and biscuits. But instead of the coffee Jack ordered she set down a glass of milk.

"You know coffee will stunt your growth, kid. And that would be a real problem for you."

Still not raising her head, Jack said, "Okay."

After eating, she went for a walk. She passed the Bank of Sanford at the corner of Park and Oak, and then continued down the street, looking in shop windows. The general store was on Oak in the middle of the block. In the window was a plain but elegant black dress, much fancier than the one she had worn the day she picked up the money. Jack went into the store and asked the salesclerk how much the dress was.

"More than you have, son."

"I want it for my momma and I've got the money," Jack said. With that, she pulled a wad of bills out of her pocket. The clerk immediately fetched the dress. Jack looked around and when the clerk returned, she said, "My momma will need a hat to go with that dress."

"We only have two."

Jack chose the one that covered the most hair, paid for the purchase and waited for the items to be boxed up.

"Can we ship these to your ma?" the clerk asked.

"Naw, I wanna show 'em to Cole."

It had become clear to Jack that everybody in the town of Sanford knew Cole. She saw the clerk give her a pinched look as if to say, "When Cole sees what this kid bought, he's going to send him right back here to get his money back."

Jack walked out of the store with the box under her arm. She headed for the livery stable. John Toms was nowhere in sight as she entered the stable and looked around. She quickly climbed into the loft and hid the box behind some old bridle equipment. Jack walked back to the hotel to find Cole still sitting at the table. She knew at this point that there was no getting him away until his money was gone. She stopped at the desk and said to the clerk,

"Cole wants to know the name of the bank president."

The clerk answered,

"Cole knows the bank president's name is Henry Nenon."

Then Jack asked the clerk for a piece of paper and a pen. The clerk pointed to the desk in the corner. Jack went over, sat down at the small desk, which had an inkwell in the top right-hand corner. She found paper in the slot under the desk, took hold of the pen with the large, feathered end, and began to write.

The note said,

Dear Mr. Nenon,

I will arrive at your bank at approximately 3:30 p.m. on Wednesday, September 3, 1884, to discuss a large deposit. Please keep this correspondence in strictest confidence. I will conduct my business with you and you alone.

Sincerely,

Mrs. Samuel Hamilton

Jack placed the note in one of the small envelopes, sealed it, and wrote on the outside,

"To Mr. Henry Nenon, President, Bank of Sanford."
Back out on the street Jack walked the block and a half to the bank. Just inside a clerk glared at her.

"What do you want in here, kid?"

Jack, taking care to lower her voice again, although it didn't really seem to matter, said,

"I have a message for Mr. Nenon."

"I'll give it to him," the clerk said as he grabbed for the envelope, but Jack pulled it away and said,

"No, I have to give it to him personal."

With that, Jack went over and sat in a chair. The clerk stalled a while and then finally disappeared in the back of the bank. Soon a man in a brown suit appeared in front of Jack.

"Give me the message, boy."

"Are you Mr. Nenon?"

He nodded and Jack handed him the note. The bank president tore it open, read it, and turned around and walked back into his office. The appointed time was only two hours away. Jack walked back to the hotel, found Cole still playing cards, and came around his back and stood staring at him.

"Hey, Cole, your kid wants to talk to you."

"He's not my kid."

Cole looked at Jack and said,

"Go find something to do. I'll be finished up here soon."

Even though Catherine had heard lots of stories, legends actually, about Cole's strange behavior, Jack was puzzled that this man who was so focused on their mission could suddenly change and become almost another person—one obsessed with poker.

She walked out of the saloon and back to the stable, found the box from the general store, went up the back steps of the hotel and slipped into her little room behind Cole's.

At precisely 3:00 in the afternoon, Mrs. Samuel Hamilton walked into the bank. She looked lovely in black mourning clothes. The hat's veil partly covered her face, but what could be seen was smooth, powered, and rouged. She told the clerk that she believed she had an appointment with Mr. Henry Nenon. The clerk asked her to have a seat and ran off to find the bank president. Almost immediately, Mr. Nenon appeared and ushered her back to his office.

"I'll get right to the point, Mr. Nenon. I am a recent widow and have just sold my ranch. I have the bill of sale with me. I am leaving Florida for a time and would like to leave the proceeds from the sale in your bank."

Mr. Nenon looked at the woman with a combination of anticipation and disbelief, and said,

"Certainly."

"Now, Mr. Nenon, I understand that women sometimes have difficulty with banking transactions. Especially when they try to withdraw money. Will I be having any problems?"

"Since you are a widow, absolutely not. There are laws that protect you, you know. When would you like to deposit the money?"

"Today. Right now. I have it here with me." Catherine lifted up the bag from the general store.

"And how much will we be depositing today, Mrs. Hamilton?"
"$17,000."

Still smiling over her transaction with the nonplussed Mr. Nenon, Catherine walked back around the corner to the back steps of the hotel. Making sure she wasn't seen, she got to her room, changed back into her boy clothes, and again became Jack.

Late that afternoon, Cole finally stepped onto the porch of the Sanford Hotel. Aside from a couple of catnaps when he opted out of a hand, he had been playing poker for 24 hours. And he was tired, hungry, and broke. Jack found him there talking amiably with some of the men who had been in the game. Jack sat on the railing and listened. She had one foot propped on the rail and one dangling toward the wooden floor of the porch. She said nothing as the men bantered. One of the men was standing against the rail with his hand extended, gripping the rail. The men were telling bawdy stories and the man next to Jack was laughing and stretching his arms. As his hand moved down the rail, he saw a quick movement from the corner of his eye and immediately felt a sting. As he looked down, he saw his hand had moved slightly between Jack's legs and there was a knife blade puncturing the web between his fingers. Blood trickled down to the rail and under his hand.

He bellowed,

"Why you little bastard, I'll kill you."

But as he started to lunge forward, he was made painfully aware that the knife was still catching the skin between his fingers. The other men just looked on in amazement wondering what prompted the kid to attack him. Cole sprang up as Jack pulled the knife back. Shielding Jack with his back, Cole said, "Woody, he's a kid. Let me take care of it."

By that time, Woody had pulled a rag from his pocket and was wrapping his hand. There was only a slight cut. It was clear to Woody by the look in Cole's eyes that he would have to take on both of them if he went after the boy. Woody glared at Jack and walked back into the bar. Minutes later, Jack walked into the bar, found Woody, and said,

"I'm sorry I stuck you, mister. You scared me." Jack extended her small hand. Woody stared at it a second then shook it. The other men at the bar hooted and clapped.

Jack was lying in the bed in the little room with the gun resting on her chest when she heard him come in. She knew after he'd slept a few hours he had gone out late. She could tell he was angry by the way he moved around in the next room. After a while he knocked lightly on her door and partially opened it.

"Don't shoot me. I just want to talk to you," he said as he stood in the doorway.

"What you did was stupid, but I guess you couldn't help it."

She replied, "What are you doing up here? Why aren't you down there losing all of your money?"

"I did lose all of my money. Are you up to heading toward Cassadaga tomorrow morning?"

"You're the one who played cards for 24 hours and came out broke. And you're calling me stupid?"

He sat down on the small wooden chair against the wall. He told her that once he started doing some things like drinking or gambling he couldn't stop.

"That's why I don't drink."

They talked for a while, and she felt like he was himself again. Later, she told him about the appointment with the bank president. She thought he would be furious, but he just laughed and said, "You sure seem to have a need to get yourself killed."

They talked a few more minutes and then Jack said she needed to go to sleep.

As Cole got up to leave, Catherine reached under the pillow and said,

"Here's the money I owe you." She handed him a wad of bills totaling $2,000. He took the money and said, "Good night."

CHAPTER THIRTY

DEAL, OR NO DEAL?

• • •

When Jack woke up the next morning, she washed her face in the little sink in the corner of the room. She had noticed it the night before, but thought it was a cabinet of some kind. There was no plumbing there, but after discovering what it was, she had poured fresh water into the tank above it. Now, when she turned on the metal faucet, the water flowed into the small basin. When she finished washing she closed the lid, causing the sink to tip and drain into a pan in the bottom.

She dressed and then knocked on Cole's door. He wasn't there. She went downstairs and found him playing poker in the bar. It was 8:30 in the morning.

She ate breakfast in the little café and then went back to her room to write. Instead of sitting at the desk, she lay down on the bed with her pencil and paper. Feeling unwell, she soon fell asleep.
The sound of voices awakened her. It was early in the afternoon. She listened for a moment and knew that Cole was in his room and he wasn't alone. She heard the unmistakable sound of a woman's seductive voice. Without thinking, she jumped out of her bed and

burst into the room to find the two of them sitting on Cole's bed, talking.

"When are we leaving, Cole? It's time to go."

She thought her voice was even, but it was high pitched and more "girl-like" than she had allowed it to be since they started this odyssey. Looking both angry and suspicious, the woman jumped up and said, "I guess I'd better get back downstairs."

Cole said, "No, you stay. Just give me a minute to talk to Jack." As he said this, he pushed Jack back into her room and slammed the door closed behind them.

"What the hell is wrong with you? That was really stupid."
"Oh, and you're not being stupid? I'm tired of waiting, Cole. Either we go now, or the deal's off and I want my $2,000 back."

"The deal can't be off because some of the money's gone. I'll calm her down and get rid of her. Then we'll make some plans."

Jack said, "Wait a minute." Then she reached under the bed and brought out the box holding the dress and hat she had bought the day before. She handed it to Cole.

"See if this will help."

After Cole left the room with the box under his arm, Jack lay back down on the bed. Her back was hurting and the pain and burning

she had been experiencing off and on since that awful day had
returned with a vengeance.

Two hours later Cole and Jack were back on their horses, headed
for the riverbank.

CHAPTER THIRTY-ONE

THE ST. JOHNS

• • •

The history of the north part of Central Florida is dominated by the majestic St. Johns River, sometimes described as "the great highway of the peninsula." The river opened Central Florida to northern contact by an inland water route more than 200 miles long. The widest part of the river was called Lake Monroe. Sanford sat at the southern edge of the lake. To the north, the community of Enterprise enjoyed a reputation for having exclusive retreat hotels that were among the early destinations for wealthy northerners who arrived by boat before the trains came.

Ferries large enough to accommodate horses and buggies traveled across Lake Monroe from Sanford to Enterprise several times a day. Each ferry could carry passengers and up to two wagons from one riverbank to the other. The owner of a four-horse team paid one dollar to get him, his horses, and his wagon across the river. A rider with a saddle horse paid 75 cents, and foot passengers paid 25 cents. Because a dollar was a hard-working man's pay for a day, it was rare that a cowboy or farmer would make the trip. In that respect, the river served to separate Central Florida's haves and its have nots.

Catherine and Cole stood on the ferry, holding the horses' reins as the pilot pulled away from the dock. All at once, they saw a horse and buggy rapidly coming around the bend and up to the dock. There was a lone woman in the buggy. Jack thought the pilot might go back for her, but she wasn't there to board. She was there to say goodbye. The woman climbed down from the buggy and ran to the dock. As she waved her white handkerchief lovingly at Cole, Jack could see that it was the woman from the hotel, outfitted very demurely in Mrs. Samuel Hamilton's dress and hat.

As they neared the other side of the river, Enterprise's preeminent hotel, the elegant Brock House, proudly stood directly in front of them facing the lake. The barge docked at the hotel's pier. Seemingly unimpressed, the two mounted their horses and headed toward the trail leading to Cassadaga, about a day's ride north of Enterprise.

Jack's body was on fire, but she managed to stay in the saddle for about five miles. But as they slowly rode the horses single file through a heavily wooded area Cole saw her slumping in the saddle. They stopped and when he touched her, he felt the heat of her fever. He asked if she could ride any farther and she said she wasn't sure. They rode to a clearing, where he laid her bedroll on the ground, just in time for her to collapse on top of it.
As a Methodist circuit rider, Cole had covered the entire Central Florida area, from Yeehaw Junction to DeLand. He knew the landscape. He knew the weather. And he knew the people.

About 10 miles northeast of Enterprise was a Seminole Indian outpost. Living next to the outpost was a small group of Catholic nuns. They weren't cloistered, as such, but they lived in a semi-cloistered way in an abbey consisting of a series of concrete structures close to the chickees, inhabited by the Indians. They had earned an excellent reputation for caring for the sick, as well as teaching in ways the Indians could accept.

Father Felix Prosper Swemberg, a Roman Catholic priest, had started the Catholic mission outpost. Swemberg was born in Cassel, France, near the border with Belgium. He studied theology and medicine in France before moving to Topeka, Kansas, in the mid 1860s. He served churches at several frontier settlements, often stepping in to resolve disputes between Indians and settlers. He built churches, schools, and missions from Kansas to the Texas panhandle. Henry Sanford invited Father Swembergh to come to Florida and start a Catholic colony.

Father Swembergh wasn't in Florida long before he came down with yellow fever and died. But he was able to start the colony east of Sanford, which exists to this day, and he helped Sister Magdalene establish the mission post prior to the smallpox outbreak.

A woman of considerable medical and organizational skills, Sister Magdalene continued to run the mission after the Father's untimely death. And she won the hearts and the respect of the small group of outcast Seminoles by nursing most of them through their own smallpox outbreak.

When Cole knew that Jack could ride no further, he climbed down from his horse, carefully lifted her from her bedroll and carried her to his own horse. He sat Jack in his saddle and then climbed on behind her. They rode that way, with her cradled in his arms, and her horse trailing behind until they reached the outpost.

Sister Magdalene was standing in the doorway of the abbey as Cole and Jack rode up. She had seen them coming from half a mile away and she recognized Cole. When they came closer, it became obvious to the nun that someone was injured or ill. Even though Sister Magdalene appeared to be a severe, disciplined person, which she was, she had great affection and admiration for Cole. She knew the good and the bad about him, and like the Indians, she called him *Fallen Angel.*

"Bring the child in here," she said, opening the door of the abbey. By then, another nun and one of the Indians were helping Cole and Jack down from the horse.

Cole replied, "This is not a child. This is Catherine Hamilton."

Cole left Catherine with the two others while he went to talk with Sister Magdalene. He told her everything.

The sister told Cole she would keep Catherine until she was out of danger, but that he could not stay. Cole unsaddled Catherine's horse, took the saddle bag containing cash that Catherine had kept for herself and a few other personal items, and asked the sister to save them until Catherine was well enough to have them. Then he mounted his horse and disappeared.

Catherine lay in a feverish coma for four days. Occasionally she drifted to consciousness and was sure she had died and was being cared for by angels. On the fifth day, she woke up enough to ask where she was. She remembered being on the barge with Cole, but not much after that. As Sister Magdalene nursed Catherine she filled in the empty places in her mind.

CHAPTER THIRTY-TWO

GERMS

• • •

In the year that Cole was a circuit-riding Methodist preacher, he visited the Seminole Indians at the outpost and usually stayed several days. Although Sister Magdalene was leery at first, she grew to understand his quirks and the two gradually developed mutual respect that fostered a deep friendship. Above all, their connection was based on their respective attitudes about medicine, which were very much alike--but contrary to the prevailing views of the time. They were both healers and Cole suspected that Sister Magdalene, like himself, was a *wounded* healer.

On his third visit to the outpost, Cole camped a half-mile away on the Dragoon Trail that led from Fort Kingsbury to Smyrna on the coast. It was late afternoon, and he was just settling in when a young Seminole boy not more than 10 or 11 years old rode up on a cracker horse. The boy knew Cole and said in near perfect English, "Sister wan you come."

Cole asked him what the sister wanted, but the boy would only repeat, "Sister want you come."

They rode off together the short distance to the outpost. What he found when they reached their destination was a very agitated half-breed woman, pacing up and down in front of the chapel. She was speaking rapidly, almost in a chant, sometimes in Creek and sometimes in English. She was holding a Bible, as if she was quoting from it but she was, for the most part, spouting gibberish.

Sister Magdalene and the other sisters were standing at a distance watching the woman. When she saw Cole, she walked up the trail to meet him.

"Thank you for coming, Cole. Some of the Seminoles thought perhaps you could help us."

Then, glancing at the woman she said, "She's been doing this for 12 hours."

As Cole and the boy climbed down from their horses, he asked the sister, "Why? What got her started?"

"She thinks she's Jesus."

Cole knew better than to laugh. The three nuns and the handful of Seminoles standing around the woman looked exhausted. The woman, on the other hand, still had a fiery look in her eyes, as if she could go on indefinitely.

"How did she come to this, sister? Where'd she get the Bible?"

Seeing that Cole was trying hard not to enjoy this trying situation, the sister replied, "Not from us. It's you Protestants who recommend reading the Bible. We discourage it, you know."

"Seriously, Cole, the woman lost her entire family to typhoid and has been depressed ever since. A few days ago, an evangelist came through and took her under his wing. I thought at first he may have done her some good, but he left last night and she started this at daybreak. We've tried reasoning with her and even wrestling her to the ground, but she appears to have unusual physical strength. At first she drew a crowd. Then we had to shoo away the children, who were throwing rocks at her. Later we thought we could just wait it out because she's obviously very ill. But it's time to do something."

Cole sat down on a rock and began to think. He unsuccessfully tried to remember something in the Bible that might get the woman's attention. But as his mind drifted and he found himself engulfed in the lush plant life of his surroundings, he thought of the Seminoles' strong belief in herbal medicine. Tribal doctors believed that medicinal plants could heal everything from alligator bites to bad dreams. But there were no tribal doctors at this outpost and he discarded the idea of trying to sedate the woman with them.

Central Florida's multiple waterways have idyllic pools, many of which sprout springs. The springs were constantly enticing patients from the north with their promise of health and healing. Cole wasn't sure what to believe about the healing power of the springs, but he knew that the Seminoles believed strongly in the mineral water therapy for melancholia, just as the ancient Greeks and

Romans did. He also knew that some alkaline springs in Florida and Georgia were said to contain small portions of natural brines and lithium—elements known to have a calming effect on those who were suffering from certain kinds of agitation.

Cole and the boy soon rode off. When they returned an hour or so later, the woman was still at her post delivering her unintelligible soliloquy.

With water bags they had filled at the nearest spring, Cole edged close to the woman. She ignored him. He tried speaking to her, explaining that the bags contained the healing waters of the springs, but she continued her pace. Exasperated, Cole jumped in front the woman and, as he dumped the chilly contents of the water bag over her head, he yelled,

"Jesus, I am John the Baptizer, and I baptize you."

She stopped short, looked at him and fainted dead away.

Cole traveled back to his campsite, but returned to the small abbey the next morning to see how she was doing. She was still sleeping and continued to do so for another eight hours.

A few months later, Cole visited with Sister Magdalene and inquired about the woman. To his surprise the sister told him that, not only had she had no more episodes, but also, her depression was gone.

When he asked the nun what she thought was keeping the woman well, the sister replied, "The spring water."

After the water cure, Cole and Sister Magdalene continued to enjoy their medical chats. They often discussed the Hippocratic Oath, "First do no harm" and debated its meaning in different situations. This was a time when crude methods were still being used in sparsely populated areas. Many country doctors still did not wash their hands, and amputation was still often used for serious wounds.

One night Cole traveled with a country doctor who went from treating a man trapped under a wagon wheel to treating a scarlet fever victim to delivering a baby –while only wiping his hands in between visits on an old rag in the back of his buggy. Even some of the Florida crackers themselves, from time to time, mentioned to Cole that it seemed as though a person's chances of staying alive improved when the doctor *didn't* show up.

Cole and Sister Magdalene both believed that germs and infections could be spread from one place to another and from one person to another. Consequently, they believed that keeping the patient and themselves clean, and helping the patient drink clean water and eat small amounts of nourishing food were the most important ways to advance the healing process.

Cole found it interesting that Sister Magdalene's ideas about healing came mostly from the Old Testament. She had not read the Bible until after she was a fully ordained nun. Once she did, she was impressed by how much sense the laws in the book of Leviticus made to her.

One evening, as they were sitting in front of the abbey before supper, the nun asked Cole to read a few chapters to her from the frayed, beaten up Bible that she knew he carried in his saddlebag. As he read, Cole was astonished, once more, by the Hebrew teachings. There were stories about blood contamination, infectious skin disease, boils, burns, and other medical conditions. There were two chapters on mildew–a constant presence in humidity-laden Florida. Both Cole and Sister Magdalene suspected that mildew had something to do with the frequent lung infections they encountered.

Sister Magdalene then told Cole something he would never forget. Twenty years earlier, when she was in a convent in Eastern Europe, an older nun had relayed to her a story that had originated in Russia. There were many villages scattered on a remote mountainside. When the plague of 1771 finally reached the area, it infiltrated one of the villages and slowly spread up and down the mountain until every inhabitant eventually became infected and died. That is, everyone except for a small ghetto of Jews who had been ostracized by the other Russians. As the plague rolled down the mountainside and back again, the Jews in the little ghetto remained uninfected. Sadly, when word got out about this miraculous occurrence, they all—even the children—were executed for being witches. Later on, those who thought about it rationally realized the reason had to be that they were keeping the Law. Their God and their isolated lifestyle had protected them.

CHAPTER THIRTY-THREE

RUSTLERS & RAILROADS

• • •

The first white man to permanently settle in the center of Florida's Orange County was Aaron Jernigan—a rancher and Indian fighter from South Georgia. He arrived in 1843 with 700 head of cattle. In the 1870s, Central Florida was still untamed and primarily occupied by Indians. Raising cattle was the main occupation for the few white men who ventured into the region, and a cowboy's life was hard.

As the decade progressed and ranching began to make some men rich, a few unscrupulous ranchers began doing whatever they could to stay on top. Rustling became commonplace and—for the most part—whatever it took to win in any situation was accepted, and outlaws were everywhere.

On July 21,1875, twenty-two men cast ballots to incorporate the two-miles-square city of Orlando, which had 85 residents. The town elected its first marshall, James W. Williams, who was killed in a gun battle a year later. Outside the city limits, range wars and vigilante justice continued to serve as law.

In 1881, with a population of 200, Orlando got its first railroad station and that brought on rapid growth. But it also upset the cattlemen. For instance, if a cattleman thought the train was going too fast for his cattle to get out of the way, he might place cross ties over the tracks and set them on fire. In addition, men boarded moving trains and shot passengers outright to scare northerners from coming into the area.

South of Orlando, around the rodeo town of Kissimmee, a well-organized band of rustlers terrorized the ranchers, themselves. In 1884, the infamous gang, the McCracken boys stole cattle all the way to the 300,000-acre Mormon Ranch, 30 miles to the east.

At that time, in the north end of Orange County, Robert Barton was the man to be feared by ranchers and railroad passengers alike. Barton not only was continuing to wreak havoc with the railroad, but county leaders constantly got word of crooked land deals, intimidation, and even cold-blooded murder involving Barton. The final straw was the disappearance of Sam and Catherine Hamilton, especially when it was learned that Robert Barton now owned the Hamilton Ranch or what was left of it. It was a mystery as to why Barton would burn down the large cypress ranch house, but that's what the cowboys found when they returned from driving the Hamilton cattle to Tampa.

The county brought in a special prosecutor from Tallahassee. His first assignment was to gather enough evidence against Robert Barton, not only to get rid of him for good, but also to demonstrate that a new day was coming to Central Florida. And it would be coming by rail.

CHAPTER THIRTY-FOUR

THE PROSECUTOR

• • •

Benjamin Elliott listened to the rancher's wife as she laid out her sad story. It was only one variation of the many versions he had listened to for the past six weeks. They all had the same theme: extortion, brutality, murder, and extreme intimidation. The other thing they all had in common was Robert Barton. But few of these ranchers were ready to come before a jury—not while Barton himself was sitting across the room, looking them in the eye.

After the woman left his small office on Church Street in Orlando, the prosecutor sat with his hands cupped over his face. He and his men had heard scores of testimonies, and to his surprise, far more women than men had come forward with their accounts of being mistreated and swindled by Robert Barton. Sharing with the prosecutor what they had endured apparently had a cathartic effect on the women. And the prospect of restitution outweighed the humiliation of telling their stories of loss.

Ben had one hope and that was to find Catherine Hamilton. When he started his investigation, he assumed she was dead. Then a bartender from Chuluota told them that Barton's men were looking for her. Two of them, drunk out of their minds, had told the bartender that she took off with Barton's $20,000, after burning down her own house. After that Ben's detectives scoured all of Central Florida for her and, to his surprise, they discovered that she had deposited most of the money in a bank in Sanford only three days after the fire. But after that, she seemed to vanish into thin air. Ben looked up, as one of his associates rushed into the office. "I think we've found Catherine Hamilton!"

"Where?"

"A woman who fits her description is teaching school at an Indian outpost in Volusia County."

CHAPTER THIRTY-FIVE

THE WISDOM OF THE DREAM
• • •

C atherine spent the first two weeks at the abbey lying in a
tiny dark room on a mattress made of straw. Besides the
infection that had permeated her body, she was suffering
from exhaustion and a depression she had not allowed to surface
since that awful day. But at the same time, she felt safe. Sister
Teresa, a young nun assigned to care for Catherine, bathed her in
cool water, fed her soup from a wooden bowl, and sang and talked
to her in spite of Catherine's silence. She was in another world.

After she and Sam had moved to the ranch, and she had become
frustrated with her life, she began to have the same perplexing
nightmare—over and over. After Cole had expressed his take on the
dream's meaning—it had gone away—until now. It was back.

In Catherine's nightmare, she was in a house with many rooms.
She felt overwhelmed and frightened, as if she were in a strange
and alien land. Then she heard a weak cry. Perhaps it was a cat or
some other animal? But, no, it sounded more like a baby. But she
had no baby, and she never would have one. She began searching
the rooms, but there were so many, and the baby's cry was so weak.

And then she opened a door and there it was, lying in a crib. She suddenly realized that this was her baby but, somehow, she had forgotten about it and had not fed it. As she stood there, paralyzed with fear and guilt, looking at the neglected, starving infant, the dream would end and she would awaken with a start.

The night on the trail, when she woke up in a cold sweat with Cole shaking her and asking her not to shoot him, she had sat up and told him about the dream. Throwing his head back, laughing, he had asked, "Don't you know you're the baby?"

And now in this tiny, safe room, she finally was able to allow herself to grieve and start to sort out her life, while others took care of her. The nuns were kind and skilled and, under the direction of Sister Magdalene, her body and her spirit began to mend. Sister Teresa did not question Catherine about what had happened to her, and Sister Magdalene never even inquired about Cole. The saddlebag with Catherine's money inside was on the floor in the corner of the room the entire time.

The third week at the abbey, Catherine began moving about the room. One morning, she woke up to find clothes on the wooden chair in the corner. She got dressed and ventured outside. The sun beating down made her swoon, but she gradually worked her way around the little compound.

There were places in the abbey she was not invited to enter, but gradually, she began helping prepare meals and, in the evenings, she helped gather vegetables from the garden. She spent most of her time reading and writing. She used the journal she always had with her, and when that was full, Sister Teresa gave her more paper. As she became aware of the rhythms of the prayer and worship times, she began to discover a new calmness within herself. Not one word was ever spoken to Catherine about the windfall in the small chapel's offering box.

CHAPTER THIRTY-SIX

SEMINOLE LIFE

• • •

By this time, the vast majority of the Seminoles had been settled, by law, much further south in the Big Cypress swamp. But a small band of families was stopped in its tracks when smallpox swept through its ranks. The tribe's young men had been taken ahead of the others to the Big Cypress settlement on the edge of the everglades in South Florida, leaving the women and children and older men behind. When smallpox swept through, the weakest of them died in the epidemic, leaving the small beleaguered extended family groups. Other than that, it was a typical Seminole community of palm thatched houses called chickees. These were open sided buildings suited to the typically hot and humid climate.

A handsome people, the women wore long full skirts made of brightly colored calico or gingham in patchwork designs. They wore multi-stranded necklaces made of shell or trade beads and sometimes rows of silver coins were sown on their dresses. They were and still are a poor and humble, but beautiful, people.

But that was not always the case with the Seminoles. The forerunners of the Seminole Tribe of Florida, the Lower Creeks, can be traced back at least 12,000 years, and some myths say that the people were molded from mud at the beginning of time. This correlates with the belief of some Christians that God created the earth by putting the Garden of Eden in Florida.

A strong and stubborn people, the Seminoles never signed an official treaty with the United States, and to this day, they supposedly are still at war with the government. Unbeknownst to them, however, they were doomed when the first white man set foot on American soil. The first Europeans brought with them new diseases like measles, smallpox, and the common cold, which killed thousands of these proud indigenous people. And later the wars came.

The best known of the Seminole resistance leaders was Osceola. He was fierce, but what fueled his reputation was his bloodthirsty taste for theatrics. But he wasn't alone in that area. When Osceola died, at age 34, the army doctor Frederick Weedom removed the Indian's head before his burial and placed it in the window of his St. Augustine drugstore where it was admired by civilized white folks for years!

On Christmas Day of 1837, 1,000 troops, under General Zachary Taylor, marched against fewer than 500 Seminoles, led by Alligator Abiaka in the battle of Okeechobee. When it was over, 26 of the 37 dead were U.S. soldiers, mostly revered Missouri volunteers. But the Indians never really had a prayer in saving their land. In 1838, the Trail of Tears forced 16,000 Cherokees to Oklahoma from the east. Two thousand died along the way. About 3,000 Seminoles, including fierce fighters like Alligator Abiaka and Wild Cat Coachoochee, also were relocated from Florida to Oklahoma.

In 1884, the nuns from St. Joseph's were sent by Father Swemberg to minister to this small band north of Lake Monroe comprised of women, children, and a few old men. The group would not have survived without the nuns.

The abbey was located only several hundred yards from the lonely renegade Seminole village. Catherine occasionally ventured out with Sister Teresa to teach the Indian children in a little chickee in the middle of the village. Catherine enjoyed watching the women grind corn with wooden mortar and pestles.

The mortar was hollowed out by charring the center of a wood log and the carved pestle was purposely left heavy above the handle to make it easier to grind the hard, dried corn. The Seminole women used the corn meal to feed their families, but the nuns made arrangements to have some of it sold, and purchased a small amount of it for themselves.

Catherine gradually learned the language well enough to lead the children in singing and eventually began doing some of the teaching herself.

And every day she grew stronger in mind and spirit.

CHAPTER THIRTY-SEVEN

THE SEARCH PAYS OFF

• • •

Ben Elliott traveled all day in his horse-drawn buggy to get to the area once known as Snow Station that now was the town of Altamonte Springs.

Taking its name from the Spanish words for "high hill" and the springs nearby, Altamonte Springs was born when five investors from Boston purchased 1,200 acres near the Snow Station depot. The Bostonians formed the Altamonte Land, Hotel, and Navigation Company, built a grand hotel on one of the area's beautiful lakes, and then laid out a village of winter houses for wealthy northerners. What separated the wealthy northerners from the homesteaders and ranchers was that the rich didn't actually live in Florida. They came, built their fabulous homes and hotels, stayed for the five or six months of perfect weather each year, and then returned to the north. The cowboys, merchants, and farmers were left to fight crime and deal with the area's burgeoning growth and change.

Cole and Catherine had steered clear of the area when they were running from Robert Barton, as Catherine had recognized at least one of Barton's men from her hometown. She was not about to take the chance of one of them looking at Jack and seeing Catherine. Ben spent the night at the great new Altamonte Springs Hotel, on Lake Orienta—one of five beautiful lakes in the chain. He had dinner that night with one of the Bostonians, who filled him in on what he knew about Catherine and her father.

Dinner at the Altamonte Hotel was a grand experience. There was no better place to see and be seen in Altamonte Springs. And the food was outstanding. Some of the lovely three-story homes in the area were built without kitchens because the winter visitors preferred to take all their meals at the hotel. Horse-drawn trams brought visitors from the train station and even carried local residents from their homes to the hotel for dinner. Meat was shipped in from New York and Boston; fish came from Tampa Bay; and fresh vegetables were grown in the hotel garden. Local farms supplied eggs and poultry, and pure spring water flowed from the ground. In addition to the dining room, the hotel boasted a billiard room, barber shop, and livery stable.

After a long night of cognac, cigars, and talk about Catherine, Ben slept late the next morning and didn't continue his journey until noon. After a few hours on dirt roads with dust half-blinding him, he was relieved somewhat by rain that came with a vengeance. The rainstorm lasted for 10 minutes, only to reveal the blazing sun again. Ben arrived at Sanford—tired, dirty, and wearing damp underwear, so he spent the night in the Sanford Hotel.

Benjamin Elliott was not an outdoorsman by any stretch of imagination. He was a cultured man with cultured tastes. His manner of dress was exquisite and, whenever possible, he stayed indoors. He often thought that, if there could ever be a way to cool the air indoors, Florida might be a tolerable place to live.
Ben had heard about an Apalachicola doctor who invented a kind of ice machine in 1851 to speed the recovery of his patients with yellow fever and malaria. He understood it as a high-pressure steam engine that absorbed the heat of hot water to create ice, but the inventor had gone broke. To Ben's knowledge, there was no artificial way of cooling Florida's steaming-hot air, which meant he was not planning to settle here for an extended period of time.

When Ben was 12 years old, he knew that law would be his career. He loved the law. He understood that, without it, no civilized society could exist. After graduating from law school (third in his class), he immediately was accepted into a prestigious legal firm in Atlanta. He was set with a large dark-paneled office and a number of cases.

Every Friday afternoon at preciously 4:00 p.m., Ben and one or two other associates were invited to have brandy with the firm's partners. Actually, this was not an invitation. The assumption was that he would be there—period. They sat in the conference room with the long gleaming table and discussed—informally, of course—what they could do to keep things in the South, and particularly in Atlanta, just the way they were; or possibly, how they could turn the clock backwards. For them, the Civil War had not ended. And certainly it had not changed anything in their minds. Ben immediately felt like an outsider in the law firm. He had no interest in this ongoing conversation, and even began to lose interest in his cases which for the most part, were all about protecting rich white people from Atlanta. It took him almost a year to figure out what he wanted to do. But when it came to him, he knew. He wanted to prosecute! Not only that, but when he was honest with himself, he knew he wanted to prosecute many of the people he now worked for—those he was hired to defend!

Ben became an excellent prosecutor. Tall and well built, he commanded the courtroom. But Ben's power was generated by his intelligence and by, to his mind, a need to right wrongs.

The third morning of his journey, Ben boarded the ferry with his horse and buggy and crossed Lake Monroe into Enterprise. From there, he traveled to the abbey. Sister Magdalene greeted him in her small office just inside the massive gates. After carefully explaining his reason for being there, Ben sat silently and looked through the open window as Sister Magdalene considered his request. Ben had told the nun the story of Robert Barton's rampages in Orange County, and the particularly brutal details of what had happened to Sam and Catherine Hamilton. He carefully explained that, to make sure this man would be dealt with in a manner that would bring justice to the people of Orange County, he needed Catherine's cooperation.

When Catherine had finished with the children for the day, she walked with Sister Teresa back to the abbey. She loved being with these children. She loved watching them play a game with a ball and sticks that looked remarkably like the game of lacrosse she had seen in England, albeit, with one small difference. When one of the

Seminole children's teams was falling behind, the other team always would reverse their strategy to help the losing team catch up.

Sister Magdalene was waiting at the entranceway when they arrived back at the abbey and invited Catherine into her office. Catherine was not surprised when she heard the story of the unexpected visit from Benjamin Elliott. Three weeks before, a small religious group had come to work with the Indians for a few days. They had left behind a newspaper and one of the children had brought it to the classroom. In it was an article about Benjamin Elliott being part of the Orange County clean up, and his determination to see that Robert Barton and everyone associated with him was either hanged or in prison.

Benjamin Elliott walked into the office and saw the small woman staring out the window. She was wearing a white shirt and long, flowing black skirt. Her skin was tanned and, even though she was very thin, she looked healthy. Her hair was pulled up in back, but ringlets cascaded around her face and neck. Other than that, she looked remarkably like a young boy.

He introduced himself and told her why he was there. "I need your testimony in order to be sure Barton and his men are put away for good."

To his surprise, she was agreeable. Looking straight into his eyes she said, "I think my goal in running away was to get to Cassadaga and somehow find some sort of spiritual power and at the same time find somebody who would be willing to go back with me to kill Barton and the others. I just felt as if I couldn't go back to

Boston until I had done this for Sam. But I know now it was crazy to think that way."

She went on to say, "I guess it took getting really sick and lying in a bed surrounded by nuns to get me thinking straight. Over the last few weeks, I've been thinking and praying about what's the right thing to do. And as I've grown stronger in my body and my mind, I've realized I'm up to it."

Ben was not a particularly religious man, so he didn't quite know what to think about what he'd just heard. Was Catherine a strong, grounded woman who would make a credible witness? He couldn't be sure until they talked further.

He told Catherine she would have to tell him everything that happened that day, as well as what led up to it, and then account for her time since then.

After three hours in the little room, they both felt drained. Ben, however, knew he had a strong witness and Catherine agreed to leave with him the next day.

Early the next morning, the horses were fresh and the buggy was ready to go. The night before, Catherine had said her goodbyes to the Seminoles and had expressed her gratitude to each of the sisters. As they started on their journey, Catherine asked Ben if they might stop for just a few minutes at the bank in Sanford. There was something she wanted to pick up. Just before leaving she had left her last $500 in the small offering box in the chapel. It would be several days before the sisters would find the money.

CHAPTER THIRTY-EIGHT

COMPLEXITY & COMPANIONSHIP

• • •

W hen Benjamin Elliott, already a well-known attorney, was called to Orange County to be the prosecutor, the first thing he had to do was to find a home for his wife and two children. He called his old friend, Nathaniel Bradlee, an architect and civil engineer from Boston, who was beginning to develop resort property in Florida with a group of friends. He was one of the founders of the Altamonte Land, Hotel, and Navigation Company.

Most of the upscale towns that were springing up in Central Florida in the late 1800s typically took form around a rambling wood-frame hotel with verandas, filled with rocking chairs and visitors from the north. Lovely homes of the most well-to-do visitors were built near the hotel.

Mr. Bradlee was able to find Ben a home similar to the ones he was building in Altamonte Springs. This particular house was located about five miles north of Orlando in the middle of a pine forest. There also was a barn and a pen for horses. The Queen Anne style house was a three-story structure with eleven rooms. It featured patterned shingled siding on the third floor, a hexagonal tower, and a beautiful gingerbread veranda. The basic shape of the house was known as "Greek cross," with interesting details featured all along the exterior. The first floor had a grand salon—some 35 feet long—with a carved cornice and fireplace, three gingerbread arches under the grand staircase, wainscoting, and French windows. Off the salon were two sets of double doors: one opening into the blue parlor for ladies and the other to the library for gentlemen. Ben loved the house the instant he saw it and knew that Margaret would love it too.

Ben loved his wife. The passion he felt the first time he'd seen her had never left him. And at times, it rose to new heights that frightened him. Even when she was difficult and made him extremely angry, the emotions seemed to feed his creative energy and make his life even better.

But the co-joined twins of genius and madness visited Margaret's mind often. And, since the twins were identical, even she could not tell them apart. At parties and other social gatherings, she could be either witty and charming or outrageously inappropriate and sullen. And Ben never could quite anticipate which side of her would emerge at any given time. But, in every part of her life, when things were good, they were very, very good.

Margaret had been the one to encourage Ben to leave the security and privilege of the law firm and seek the challenging roll of prosecutor. Whether they were home alone, or dining with the governor, Ben found Margaret to be the most stimulating person he knew. At times, when she embarrassed him in public or stayed in her room for days on end, not speaking to him or anyone else, he vaguely questioned the relationship. However, he knew she was an addiction he could never give up. And she knew it, too. That's why Margaret was not threatened in the least when Ben suggested that Catherine stay with them.

Margaret trusted Ben. He loved her and she knew it. She also was aware that loving her drained him. He would not have had the sexual energy to find solace in another women, even if he wanted to. And he did not want to. Margaret was exciting and aggressive in and out of bed—always in search of new ways to delight him— and exhaust him. So, she had no qualms about Ben inviting the intriguing Catherine to stay in their home. Ben thought Margaret might even be delighted with Catherine's company. And he was right. It wasn't long before Margaret and Catherine discovered that the most significant thing they had in common was not their beauty, their superb intellect, or their unending curiosity about life. It was that they both were fish out of water.

On the long trip back to Orlando, Ben and Catherine discussed how she would be introduced. It was important that her identity remain a secret for the time being. The secrecy was not only for Catherine's personal safety. Ben felt strongly that her testimony should be a surprise to the jury. Catherine was born Mary Catherine Richardson, so it was decided that her name now would be Mary Richardson. Margaret would call her "Sis," in hopes that most people would just assume the two women were sisters.

Margaret already had heard exciting stories about "Catherine Hamilton." And as predicted, she and Mary Catherine liked each other immediately. In addition, Margaret was instantly on board with the intrigue of trying to fool people into thinking Catherine was her sister without saying she was.

Catherine moved into the spacious home and was an instant hit with the Elliott children, Little Ben and Caroline. Since they lived so far from town, Margaret recently had hired a teacher to home school the children. But she turned out to be a severe disciplinarian whose favorite saying was, "Children, life is *not* a bowl of cherries." Catherine so enjoyed being with Little Ben and Caroline that soon she was teaching them songs in French and telling them stories of faraway places. Since Margaret was constantly battling with the teacher, Mrs. Snodgrass, Catherine persuaded her to dismiss the teacher and let her teach the children for as long as she was there. It wasn't long before Margaret was sitting in the classroom herself and the four of them would go on imaginary journeys to far-off places. Then Little Ben and Caroline would write about the experience. Catherine wasn't nearly as concerned with grammar and spelling as she was with the children being able to express themselves well. And Margaret was in full agreement. Some days they had "science outings" instead of work in the classroom.

There was a world of things to discover. Catherine also helped the children learn to ride horses with assurance and ease.

When the lessons were finished for the day, Mary Catherine and Margaret enjoyed each other's company immensely. They both were complex women—big thinkers, well educated, and well-traveled. Each of them had a longing for intellectual stimulation, which women almost everywhere in those days were deprived of–most certainly in Central Florida. They developed a close companionship.

The two loved discussing books they had read independently.

When Catherine quoted to the children one day,

I am the daughter of Earth and Water, *And the nursling of the Sky,*

Margaret immediately knew that it was from Shelly. And Percy Bysshe Shelly was not the only "Shelly" they had in common. They sat on the porch one night discussing Mary Shelly's *Frankenstein,* until it became so late that Ben came out in his nightclothes and insisted they both go to bed.

At least once a week Margaret and Catherine would have Mr. Harvey, the ranch's livery man, hitch up the two small cracker horses to the buggy so they could travel to some interesting place. Sometimes by invitation, sometimes not.

CHAPTER THIRTY-NINE

WINTER PARK

• • •

It was a grand and glorious day in 1883. Francis Knowles, a man who started out manufacturing gloves in New York and then branched out into various other businesses until he had amassed a fortune, was steaming up the Oklawaha River when he ran into an old friend, Col. Franklin Fairbanks. They shared dinner and drinks and Fairbanks regaled Knowles with lavish descriptions of a particular area of Central Florida. As Fairbanks told it, the area, with its pristine lakes and great natural beauty, had tremendous development opportunities.

In less than two years, Francis Knowles relocated to Florida and built a home in Winter Park. In 1885, he became one of the founding directors of the Winter Park Company, which, in 1904, became the Winter Park Land Company.

Winter Park started as a town of wealth and prestige. Northerners brought their servants with them and, from the beginning, the Dinky Line railroad tracks were the distinct dividing line between black and white folks. Nowhere else in the country was the division so sharp. Winter Park boasted stately mansions and tiny cracker homes, but nothing in between.

On this particular Wednesday afternoon, Mr. Knowles was hurrying home because he and Mrs. Knowles were hosting the wife of the daring new Orange County Prosecutor and her sister for lunch.

Mr. Harvey drove the horses up the two-lane dirt road into the Winter Park community. For the previous two miles, one of the buggy wheels had been making a disturbing noise each time it turned. Margaret asked Mr. Harvey to stop and said, "Is the wheel in danger of coming off?"

"I don't think so Miz Margaret. But I'll see to it when I drop you and Miss Mary Catherine at the Knowles place."

"Oh, don't be silly. I see people and lovely shade trees right up the road. You just stop now and we'll wait."

Mr. Harvey wasn't happy with this idea, but he had learned a long time ago that it was useless to argue with Miz Margaret. And her sister seemed to be just as strong headed as she was.

They pulled up to the clearing where five black men sat. Mr. Harvey asked one of the men if he would help look at the wheel. In the meantime, Margaret and Catherine climbed down from the buggy and opened their parasols against the late morning sun. They marched right over and sat down on a large tree stump next to an elderly man fanning himself with a palm branch. Margaret said, "How 'do?" The old man raised his hand as though to tip his hat, but he wasn't wearing one.

"And what do you call this lovely place?" Catherine said the old man, hardly knowing how to react to these two parasol-toting white women who had, all of a sudden, invaded his territory said, "We calls it Hannibal Square, Ma'am. After the Negro what crossed the Alps."

After the three travelers boarded the buggy again, with its wheel having been tightened, Margaret said to Catherine, "I understand that there are more blacks than whites in Winter Park. Since they stay here all year while the rich white folks head north in the summer, they could certainly run this town if they so chose." The two women laughed at that prospect, as they pulled up in front of the home of Mr. and Mrs. Francis J. Knowles.

The luncheon consisted of cold soup, fish caught from the lake that morning, and fresh fruit. The conversation was light, intelligent, and witty. Then Mr. Knowles told the women the exciting news— that a college would be opening soon in Winter Park. It would be called Rollins College, and was being sponsored by the 20 or so members of the Congregationalist Church which was also made up of Methodists, Episcopalians, and Unitarians.

After discussing the new college, Margaret asked if there was a public school system for younger children and especially the black children she had seen running around where their buggy had broken down at Hannibal Square.

"Indeed, there is!" replied Mr. Knowles. "The reason you saw those children is because the school for the white children meets in White's Hall in the daytime and the black children are schooled there at night."

Because the conversation had taken the turn that it did, Mr. Knowles neglected to tell the women that he, himself, was bankrolling the new college and the new elite 250-room Seminole Hotel that already was under construction on Lake Osceola. The motto for the new hotel was to be "A Resort for Men of Wealth."

CHAPTER FORTY

FEATHERS & FRICTION

• • •

As the trial neared, life took on a different tone in the Elliott household. Ben was trying to put all his energies into preparing himself, but it wasn't easy because Margaret recently had had one of her "episodes." Several days before, she and Catherine had returned from a shopping trip to Orlando, all excited and energized. Catherine, though, was a bit concerned about Margaret's purchases. Besides the outrageous amount of money she had spent on clothes and shoes, Margaret had insisted on buying 20 gallons of green paint that someone else had "special ordered" at the general store and neglected to pick up. And no amount of arguing could talk her out of it. In fact, it seemed to make her even more determined. Catherine had never seen Margaret lash out as she did at Mr. Harvey, as he was trying to load the paint onto the wagon. Margaret just didn't believe he was moving fast enough and she, herself, got down from the buggy to help with the loading. When they arrived at home, Margaret announced that they were going to paint the interior of the house—all eleven rooms. She insisted that everyone—the cook, the nanny, the ranch hand, Mr. Harvey, and even Catherine—get a paint brush and help complete this project.

When Ben arrived at midnight, he found the house in a disastrous array of covered furniture, mirrors, and artwork stacked against the walls, and Margaret screaming at people to keep painting.

Ben looked discouraged, but not surprised, as he asked Catherine to help him get Margaret to her room. It was quite a task, but they finally accomplished it by appealing to her newfound expertise as a painting contractor. As Catherine closed the bedroom door on them, Margaret was again ranting. For the next three days, Margaret stayed in her room and saw no one but Ben. On the fourth day, she came downstairs in her robe looking completely worn out, and apologized to the household help who were still cleaning up the mess.

The trial for Robert Barton and Charles Landry was scheduled to begin on November 16th. Ben came home one night, took Catherine into the sitting room, and told her that the man she knew as Heat, the one who had beat her senseless, and the other two men had been killed by a railroad official after they shot several passengers. Ben said, "The train had hit a herd of cattle being driven to Tampa and these men became so enraged that they began shooting randomly into the passenger cars. A railroad detective shot Heat in the head. The other two died from gunshot wounds later in the day." Ben went on to explain that this had happened weeks ago, but it had taken this long to establish the fact that they were the same men. Heat was known to have worn a small leather bag containing several human teeth around his neck. After drinking a while, he had been known to empty the bag onto the bar and show off the five teeth, but he would never say where they came from. He enjoyed the conversation that evolved from his fellow drinkers' guessing. But when Heat's body was examined, the leather bag was missing. The other two men were drifters, and nobody even knew their names.

As Catherine listened to what Ben said, she was hoping in her heart that it would make her feel better. It did not.

Security was as tight as it could be in Orlando's city jail in 1885. The new jail had been constructed on Oak Street behind City Hall. But, even with that, one of the three members of the police force, Officer William Beasley, was killed trying to quell a riot.

Orlando was changing rapidly. Since 1881 when the first railroad station was built, the population had grown from 200 to nearly 2,000. And, despite everything, cattle was still king. New breeds were brought in, like Brahmas, that had resistance to Florida's insects and heat. New cattle kings like Jim Johnson, who was never seen without his neckerchief and Stetson hat, and Jake Summerlin, who was called "King of the Crackers" raised and sold larger herds every year. And there were hundreds of smaller ranchers. And cowboys—good and bad—roamed the countryside.

Rustling was still the number one crime in Central Florida, as the open range made it easy. The only way to identify your own cattle was with branding and ear cropping. There were "brand" books with hundreds of brands, because the search was always on to find that one brand that could not be altered. It seemed that every day new families, cowboys, drifters, developers, and fortune hunters came to Florida and those who were already there wondered when it would all stop.

That's why Ben Elliott had been lured to Orange County. Crime needed to be stopped if true civilization was ever to survive in the frontier. Trying and prosecuting the men who had killed Sam would send the message that the wild, lawless times would soon be a thing of the past.

On the first day of the trial, Margaret and Catherine sat in the back row of the Orange County courtroom. Ben was not happy. Even with the evidence against the men, the trial was not going well. The few witnesses Ben had called were afraid and embarrassed. They had been intimidated and cheated for so many years by these men that it was humiliating to admit it in public. And making the trip from the northern part of the country to participate in the trial was a hardship for many of the victims. That evening, Ben let Catherine know that he would call her the next day and that just about everything depended upon her testimony.

On the second day of the trial, Ben called Mary Catherine Richardson Hamilton to the stand. As the woman many thought was Margaret Elliott's sister slowly came forward, many of the people in the packed courtroom gasped. Others, including the two defendants, displayed shock because they felt sure that Catherine Hamilton was either back in Boston or dead.

Catherine was wearing a burgundy dress and plumed hat that she and Margaret had carefully chosen. Prior to this, Catherine had never worn feathers or any other bird parts. She was firmly opposed to killing birds just so women could assume their plumage. But today, she did it for Margaret, who had seemed to be so down and depressed since the painting fiasco. In addition, Margaret had assured Catherine that wearing the hat would make her feel strong. The truth was that Catherine was so shaken by the painting incident that she did not want to risk setting Margaret off again just before the trial.

Catherine's usual aversion to wearing feathers had begun when she was living and teaching in Boston, while trying nobly but miserably to establish herself as a serious writer. She had gone to New York to gather information firsthand on the deplorable conditions under which hundreds of women were working in the new and growing sweatshops. While she was touring the shops with an unsuspecting guide, she discovered the $17 million millinery industry. She watched in horror as one young woman fastened the majestic plumes from one exotic bird and then a *whole bird* to a woman's hat. The proud young man escorting Catherine through the factory rationalized this by saying, "The Florida wilderness needs to be tamed by 'civilized' people."

Although Catherine had never been able to get her exposé published, when she got to Florida and witnessed the magnificent multicolored birds flying through the Florida skies, she was repeatedly reminded of the mistreatment of the women in the sweatshops and the cruelty inflected on the beautiful flying animals.

To further confound her dedication to Florida's bird conservation, Catherine was asked years later to interview John James Audubon, the famous ornithologist. Audubon made no secret of the fact that he killed birds in great numbers. To provide models for his famous, lifelike paintings, he first shot the birds, then skinned them and mounted the skins on wire frames. This, of course, appalled Catherine. But what drove the two into a near shouting match was when Audubon continually ranted about his intense dislike for Florida. He hated the heat, flies, and mosquitoes. He was constantly afraid that alligators would eat his dog. But his biggest complaint was that the magnificent pink flamingos and the regal sandhill cranes were just too fast for him to shoot.

CHAPTER FORTY-ONE

RELIVING THE RAMPAGE

• • •

Catherine took her seat on the witness stand. Ben began by asking her why she and her husband moved to Florida. She explained the compromise between Florida and heading west, saying, "I didn't think Sam would be much of a rancher, but I loved him and wanted him to get it out of his system."

Ben said, "Tell the jury, from your standpoint, what led up to the day your husband was killed."

She told about attending a party where Robert Barton pressured Sam to sell the ranch but Sam was firm in saying no. The next week, Joe Black found two dead horses in the pen, and later, dead and mutilated cattle on the range.

"Then Barton showed up at the house one afternoon, unannounced, and told Sam that the railroad was coming soon," she continued, "and Sam was a northerner who didn't know anything about this business." She went on to testify that Barton had said it could get really ugly, and he'd better sell while he had a chance but Sam had refused.

FLORIDA, A LOVE STORY

Ben looked Catherine straight in the eye. "Tell us now, Mrs. Hamilton, what happened on the day your husband was killed."

Catherine sat up straight and took a deep breath. Margaret had assured her that the plume in the hat would help her feel tall and strong and in some silly, strange way, it did.

"We were alone on the ranch except for Naomi and Joe Black, who worked for us. The ranch hands had driven the cattle to Tampa to be shipped eventually to Cuba. Sam wanted to go with them more than anything. He thought of this ranching business as one big adventure. He was sure he was going to make a profit, and doing that would give him the success he'd been after. But, with all of the strange things that had been happening, he was worried about leaving me and the ranch so he stayed home. I wish now that both of us had gone on the drive."

Ben looked up and said, "Let me interrupt you a minute, Mrs. Hamilton. Was there ever any doubt in your mind or your husband's mind as to who was making these strange things happen?"

The defense attorney jumped up. "I object, your honor."

"Objection denied. Answer the question, Mrs. Hamilton."

"No, there was never any doubt in our minds."

Ben said, "OK, continue telling us about the day your husband was murdered."

"We were sitting in the kitchen, drinking coffee, when Barton's men burst in. They didn't say anything. Sam jumped up and the big one raised the gun he had in his hand and shot Sam in the head. Sam was lying on the floor, bleeding all over everything, so I ran over and threw myself on top of him. One of the men, the one named 'Heat' pulled me up and began beating me with his fists. When I was down, he pounded my head on the kitchen floor. I tried hard to stay conscious, but I passed out."

Ben said softly, "If you passed out, how do you know they were Barton's men?"

Catherine was not even close to crying. Rather than falling apart—the more she told the story, the more empowered she felt.

"I know because I woke up sometime later with one of them slapping my face. The other two were laughing and talking to each other like I wasn't even there. Then Heat said to the other one, 'Let's get out of here. There's nothin' more we want here.'"

"But as they headed toward the door, the big one looked over at me and said, 'Mr. Barton will be here Wednesday morning to buy your ranch. I'm guessing you'll be ready to sell, then,' and they walked out laughing."

Then Catherine told the court about crawling across the kitchen to Sam, sitting on the floor, and cradling his head in her lap for a long time. Then she went to the bedroom and found her "Road to California" quilt. Sam's Aunt Patricia had made it for them when she thought they were going out west. It was Sam's favorite.

Catherine laid it out on the floor and carefully rolled Sam on to it. Then she wrapped it around him.

"And what happened after that, Catherine?"

"I went to the door and called for Naomi and Joe Black. When they didn't answer, I kind of stumbled out to the barn. They were gone. Then I found a shovel and dug a grave under the Live Oak and buried Sam."

Catherine made no mention of Cole.

Benjamin said, "Mrs. Hamilton, it's hard to believe that you were able to do all of this. What was going on in your mind?"

"I'm not sure." Catherine answered. "I felt like I had extra strength and a strange calmness inside me. But now, I think I could have been out of my head."

"So, Mrs. Hamilton, did you sell your ranch to Mr. Barton?"

"Yes, he and Charles Landry came the next Wednesday. I sold him the ranch and left, knowing that he would kill me if I ever returned."

"Thank you Mrs. Hamilton. That will be all."

Catherine started to leave the stand, but the lawyer for Barton and Landry had jumped to his feet.

"Now, Mrs. Hamilton, you weren't alone when Mr. Barton and Mr. Landry came to your home, were you?"

Catherine looked at the lawyer but didn't speak.

"Answer the question, please," the judge said.

"No, I wasn't alone."

"Mrs. Hamilton, didn't you have a man living with you at the time? A man, with whom you were planning to run off, and, in fact, did. A man with whom you had been having an intimate relationship for a long time?"

There was silence in the packed courtroom Catherine looked at her hands and then looked at the defense lawyer.

"No, that's not exactly true."

"Then tell us, Mrs. Hamilton, what, *exactly*, is true?"

"The man showed up for the first time, as I was burying my husband. He helped me bury him. I asked him to stay and pretend to be my lover when Robert Barton showed up, so my ranch wouldn't be stolen out from under me. Then I asked him to take me to Cassadaga."

"And he agreed?"

"Yes, he agreed."

"Now, let me get this straight, Mrs. Hamilton. You expect this jury to believe that this man did all of this out of the goodness of his heart?"

"Yes, he did it out of the goodness of his heart. And I paid him."

"How much did you pay him?"

"$2,000."

There was murmuring in the courtroom. The lawyer looked at Catherine with an obvious smirk. Shaking his finger at her, he said, "We all know what's going on here." And then he said to the judge, without looking at Catherine,

"I'm finished with this witness for right now, your honor."

Then Benjamin stood up and said, "I have no more questions for Mrs. Hamilton at this time, your honor."

The feeling of empowerment that Catherine had earlier was now replaced with uncertainty. Ben had told her there was a chance that they could lose the case, but Catherine hadn't believed him—until now.

As she got up to take her seat beside Margaret, Ben said, "I'd like to call Sister Magdalene to the stand."

A small Catholic nun in the back of the room came forward to be sworn in. Catherine was once more reminded of the feeling of being surrounded by angels and her strength began to return.

After the usual introductory questions and answers, Benjamin asked,

"Sister, do you know Mrs. Catherine Hamilton?"

"Yes, I do."

"Will you tell us how you know her?"

Sister Magdalene told the jury about Cole bringing Catherine to the abbey.

"Now sister, what condition was Mrs. Hamilton in when she arrived?"

"She was near death."

"What do you mean by 'near death?' What was wrong with her?"
"She was unconscious. She was running a high fever. There was an infection in her body."

"In your opinion, Sister, how did this infection enter her body?"

Sister Magdalene looked directly at the jury.

"In my opinion, it entered her body the day she was attacked—the day her husband was murdered."

The people in the courtroom looked uneasy, as if they wanted this testimony to be over fast.

But Ben continued.

"From a sexual attack?"

"Possibly."

Ben said, "Thank you, Sister."

Ben said, "Your honor, I'm finished with this witness."

The defense attorney rose to his feet.

"Sister Magdalene, are you a doctor?"

"No."

Well, Sister, in your "expert" medical opinion could this illness have been caused by taking a lover and traveling on the road with him for several days?"

"I don't know."

"Well, I do, and I can tell you that they've seen some serious cases like this at the Blossom Inn, down on Clay Street."

Sister Magdalene had never heard of the Blossom Inn, but she had a pretty good idea where the defense attorney was going with this accusation.

But the judge said, "Sir, there will be no more testifying from you. Get on with another line of questioning."

"Now, Sister, I understand that you and the other nuns are building several new classrooms at that Indian school you have up there in Volusia County. Is that right?"

"Yes."

"So, y'all must have come into some serious money in the last few months. Did the Pope give it to you?"

Sister Magdalene looked at the defense attorney, dumbfounded. "No."

"Well, where'd it come from?"

"It was an anonymous donation."

"Sure, it was! Thank you, Sister. You can step down now."

Ben said, "I'd like to recall Mrs. Hamilton."

When Catherine was seated, Ben looked at her and asked, "Mrs. Hamilton, with how many lovers have you had in your lifetime?"

"Only one. My husband, Samuel Hamilton."

Ben sat down and the defense attorney rose.

"I have a couple more questions, Miz Hamilton."

His southern accent seemed to become more prominent as the day wore on.

"On the day you *say* you were attacked, and your husband was allegedly killed, who else was on your ranch at the time?"

"No one. Just Sam and me."

"Well, Miz Hamilton, how do we know that you're tellin' the truth? How do we know you didn't make up this whole cockamamie story? You got no proof."

For the first time, Catherine felt shaken. The attack at the ranch was common knowledge. People knew it was true, but nobody could testify for her firsthand.

She simply said, "It happened the way I said it did."

The defense attorney said he had no more questions for the witness and Catherine was asked to stand down.

As they walked from the courtroom, Ben told Catherine that she was finished, and it was all up to the jury now. But he didn't look happy. Despite the vulgar way in which the defense attorney interrogated both Catherine and Sister Magdalene, Ben was sure he managed to plant seeds of doubt in the minds of at least some jurors.

As she walked back through the heavy crowd, she saw him. He was standing in the back corner with several other cowboys. No one seemed to notice or recognize him, as Catherine moved toward the back, and he inched his way to stay in her line of vision.

Out in the rotunda, Catherine was greeted by a few people she had met since coming to Orlando. They could have been angry for having been deceived about her being Margaret's sister, but under the circumstances, they seemed to understand. During the court days, Ben had asked Catherine and Margaret to sit in the rotunda and wait for him so the three could leave together.

Catherine was heading for a bench, where she would wait for Ben, when Cole walked up. He bowed his head in greeting as though to tip his hat, but he was not wearing one.

"You look well today, Miss Catherine."

They were both aware of the people milling around close by. Catherine stuck out her gloved hand, looked at Cole and said, "Cole, I need you to do one more thing for me."

CHAPTER FORTY-TWO

BURIED IN THE BARN

• • •

Cole rode the rest of the afternoon and into early evening. He went through the little town of Oconee and, when he reached the other side, he took the right fork in the road.

The Wilsons were getting ready for bed when they heard the knock on the door.

Cole explained his mission in his quiet, persuasive manner and soon he and Mr. Wilson were in the barn with shovels. Mrs. Wilson and the children were gathered around holding lanterns with one hand and their noses with the other. No one really expected there to be much of a treasure buried in the barn.

CHAPTER FORTY-THREE

SETTING HIS TEETH ON EDGE

• • •

To the surprise of everyone in the courtroom, Ben called Catherine back to the stand. Over the loud objections of the defense attorney, she was allowed to continue her testimony.

"Mrs. Hamilton, the defense attorney has suggested that *possibly* your husband wasn't shot and that *possibly* you were not beaten senseless by the man known as Heat, alleged to be Robert Barton's hired gun. He says there is no proof. Is there?"

"Yes, there is," Catherine said followed by a persistent stirring in the courtroom.

"And what proof do you have?"

Catherine held out her hand. "It's right here."

Ben lifted from Catherine's hand a small leather pouch attached to a leather string. He walked to the judge's bench and poured the contents of the bag onto the bench. The judge stared at the five human teeth.

Ben looked back at Catherine.

"Where did you get this disgusting bag of teeth, Mrs. Hamilton?"

"I pulled it from that man's neck while he was pounding my head against the floor."

The judge had to, again, quiet the courtroom as Ben finished with Catherine's testimony. The defense attorney, obviously surprised by the turn of events stood and said, "Mrs. Hamilton, where have you been hiding this little piece of evidence all this time?"

"It was buried in my neighbor's barn."

The defense attorney pursued a few other lines of questioning, but he was not able to break Catherine's resolve. Finally, he told the court he was finished, and the judge excused Catherine from the witness stand.

But before moving, she looked at the judge and asked, "Your honor, may I say something?"

Both attorneys jumped to their feet to protest, but the judge looked back at Catherine and said, "I think you've earned that right, Mrs. Hamilton. Proceed."

"Your honor, when this happened to me, all I could think about was revenge. And not even so much revenge on the men who hurt me and killed my husband, but revenge on Robert Barton for all of the terrible things he's ever done. I wanted to go to Cassadaga in hopes of finding some way to come back and kill Robert Barton. But on the way, when I almost died, I experienced unconditional kindness and acceptance from the nuns. And in time, I decided how I really wanted to handle this and maybe even how God wanted me to handle this. When Mr. Elliott visited me at the abbey and gave me the opportunity to tell my story, I knew what I was supposed to do. I know there are lots of people, other than me, in this room who have been hurt by Robert Barton."

And then Catherine looked around the courtroom.

"I wish you could come to this box and say it all. You may think that telling your story would be almost as painful as it was for you and your families to be victimized by Robert Barton. Instead, it would make you feel both powerful and free! Soon I'll leave to go back to Boston, but if you want Florida to be a fit place to stay and raise your families, you have to get rid of people like Robert Barton."

The packed courtroom was quiet. Catherine was exhausted. Court was adjourned for the day.

Catherine sat for a moment before leaving the building. Her head was swimming. She could not believe that they didn't ask her about burning down her house. And even more surprising to her was that Cole's name was never mentioned.

CHAPTER FORTY-FOUR

GOOD VS. EVIL

• • •

G etting ready to leave the Elliotts and their stately home was not easy. Catherine loved every one of them. And she would be eternally grateful to both Margaret and Ben for changing her life for the better, each in entirely different ways. But Catherine finally would be on her way home to Boston.

After finishing her testimony, Catherine had not returned to the courtroom. Margaret had burst into her room the next evening to tell her what happened.

Barton's victims were lined up to testify. Jack Trotter, a rancher from North Orange County whom Catherine didn't know, told about how Barton and Landry had taken half of his cattle. The day after he had complained to the sheriff, his little boy was ambushed on the way home from school and part of his ear was cut off. The stories of violence and intimidation continued on into the afternoon. After that, it was as though half the county wanted to testify. In the end, Barton and Landry were sentenced to hang.

CHAPTER FORTY-FIVE

THE CONFESSION
• • •

Cole turned off the road and rode down the path toward the Altamonte Hotel, nestled among the tall pines and gracious oaks surrounding Lake Orienta. He walked inside and asked at the desk for Mrs. Catherine Hamilton. The clerk sent a boy to her room and soon Catherine appeared in the lobby. She looked stunningly beautiful. There was no pretense at being anything other than what she was a well educated, well-to-do Bostonian. Cole asked her if she would have supper with him at the Altamonte Cafe, but she told him she already had arranged for their dinner in the hotel restaurant.

They were seated in a far corner of the crowded dining room. Even so, many of the proper northern diners, who recognized them, tried not to be too obvious in their staring and tongue wagging. They ordered their dinner and then discussed the trial. Cole asked her about her stay at the abbey and she told him how it had been a life-changing experience. He told her what he had done since leaving her. She didn't broach the subject that he *had* left her, and he didn't mention it either.

As they were finishing their dinner of oysters and grilled steaks, Catherine said, "Cole, I have something I want to say to you. I'm leaving in three days and it's not likely I'll ever be back in Florida. But I want you to know how much you've meant to me."

She put her hand lightly on his, fully aware than half the room might be watching. "I want you to know that I love you."

He pulled his hand away and began moving around uncomfortably in his seat, while rearranging the silverware on the white linen tablecloth.

But Catherine continued, "I've tried to rationalize it in my mind by telling myself that my feelings for you are strictly those of gratitude for all of the things you've done for me, but I know it's more than that. Despite being full of grief and hatred, and being physically ill throughout our trip, I also felt more fully alive with you than I've ever been before. You are the most interesting man I've ever known."

She paused for a minute to see if he would respond but wasn't surprised when he didn't. Then she went on, "You are a good man, Coleman Wills. You're not a very careful man and I don't think you're going to live to be an old man, but you're good. And I'll always be grateful that I have known you and have loved you."

He said nothing for a few seconds. Then he asked a passing waiter for the check. The waiter told him the dinner had been taken care of.

Catherine was brushing her hair thinking about how she had blabbered on to Cole. She had not expected more from him than silence, but she wasn't sorry for her confession. She was sitting at the mahogany dresser in her hotel room, thinking about the little room behind Cole's at the hotel in Sanford. It had only been a few months since then, but it seemed like a lifetime ago. She was wearing a silk dressing gown over a cotton nightgown. The window was open, and she could faintly hear the music coming from the hotel dining room—the one she and Cole had been together in only half an hour earlier.

There was a soft knock at the door. She opened it without hesitation and Cole stepped into the room. They embraced and he kissed her softly. As he became conscious of the music below, he began swaying slowly and they danced that slow, rhythmic dance that lovers do.

As the sun came up, they were still there lying in each other's arms. Cole said, "If we made a child, promise me I will know about it."

"You know there is no way I can have a child."

"Promise me, anyhow."

CHAPTER FORTY-SIX

ONE MORE NIGHT

• • •

Even though Catherine already had said her bittersweet good-byes to Ben and Margaret and the children, something inside told her she had unfinished business there. She and Cole went shopping for toys and chocolates. Then Cole went to the stable and came back to the hotel with a horse for Catherine. She was waiting in her new riding clothes.

She wanted Cole to meet her dear friends before she left Florida. Reluctantly he had agreed, and they rode along the wide trail to Orlando before veering east on a trail leading to Ben and Margaret Elliott's house. As they galloped into the front yard, the children ran out to greet Catherine. She could barely climb down before they were hugging her legs and shrieking with delight. She and Cole gathered the treats they had brought, and the children led them into the house. The Elliotts had just returned from church and Ben and Margaret were in the living room, waiting for dinner to be put on the table.

"What a surprise!" Margaret exclaimed, as they came through the door. She grabbed Catherine, and hugged and kissed her, as she cried, "I thought I would never see you again, and now here you are a day later," as tears streamed down her face.

Cole was behind Catherine. She turned and said, "This is my good friend, Cole. Cole, I want you to meet my friends Ben and Margaret Elliott and their beautiful children, Little Ben and Caroline." The men shook hands and then Cole reached down and shook hands with Little Ben.

Margaret said they must eat with them and rushed off to the kitchen to ask the cook to prepare for two more.

The two women kept the conversation going at the table as they ate quail and fresh vegetables. Margaret couldn't help but notice the way Cole looked at Catherine and how Catherine comfortably let her hand rest on Cole's arm as they chatted. At one point Margaret pulled Ben into the kitchen and whispered, "This is the man, isn't it? The man who rescued her from Barton?"

Ben allowed as how it appeared that he was the man.

"Well, it's pretty clear to me that they're in love, but God help them! I've never seen two people so different—like they're from opposite ends of the earth!"

"Don't be so sure," Ben said. "They have more in common than you think."

After the children were excused from the table, Margaret—wanting to prolong the visit for as long as possible—asked Ben to tell them about a strange case he was working on.

"Let me give you a little background first," Ben said, as he pushed slightly back from the table.

"Cole, I think you'll especially find this case of interest, considering your unorthodox views on treating illness."

"South of here down toward Kissimmee but still in Orange County, there is a little Shaker community. These peaceful, non-violet Shakers had never had a run in with the law—until now.

Margaret interrupted, "Now, Ben, tell us something more about the Shakers. Maybe Catherine and Cole don't know anything about them."

"Well, I didn't know much about them either," said Ben, "until the killing."

"Just a handful of them settled down in Central Florida and formed what they called the Olive Branch Colony. Their numbers began to dwindle because they're celibate, and there are only six of them now. They have two cottages, one for the men and one for the women. Not much else is at Olive Branch except a big chicken house, a barn, a windmill, and a saw mill. But their property is full of beautifully landscaped areas with fruit trees, flowers, and vines. They make a living by producing honey, cane syrup, and pineapples, which they mostly export to Cuba."

"Well, to get on with the story, this woman, name was Sadie, turned up dead on the Shaker's property. When the sheriff got there, the first thing they did was tell him they'd given her chloroform to help her (as they said) 'pass out of her body.'"

Catherine and Cole, who had each been thinking about heading back to the hotel, were now on the edge of their seats and Catherine said, "Wait a minute before you go on. This is fascinating, but what's the background on the Shaker religion?"

Ben continued, "We did some research. Let's see if I can remember their official name. I believe it's the United Society of Believers in Christ's Second Appearing. Their beliefs go back to a 17th century group of French Protestants. They were driven out of France and settled in England where they were associated with the Quakers. Because they get so emotional that it causes them to quiver during religious exercises, they became known first as the Shaking Quakers and then just the Shakers. These people basically believe that evil springs from greed, sex, and pride. So, as far as I can tell, they don't participate in any of the three."

Catherine, a Massachusetts Episcopalian, said she had just never heard of such a thing. And she thought emotional displays were a strange way to practice one's religion.

But Cole had seen his share of Methodists who were "slain in the spirit" and evidenced it by shaking violently and even passing out. Ben continued, "But these people are God fearing and peace loving, more than anything else. They regard all forms of violence as un-Christian. That's what makes this case so strange and so difficult."

"Okay, now back to the story."

"When the sheriff heard what the Shakers had to say about the dead woman, he called it murder and arrested the six of them the next day and locked them in jail in Kissimmee. The day after that, four of them were released and one lady made bail. But Brother Charles stayed in jail. He was the one accused of the murder and there was no bail for that. When he went before the judge that morning, he made this statement: 'Before God, I think I did right, and my conscience is perfectly at ease.'"

"As I it turns out, Sadie wasn't even a Shaker. She showed up at the colony six years ago, penniless and terribly sick with tuberculosis. The doctors up north had told her that she would have only a year or so to live if she didn't get to a warmer climate, so she moved herself to Central Florida. After a few months, her money ran out and she had no place to go. She knew the Shakers were good people, so she stood on their doorstep and begged to be taken in—thinking she only had a short time to live. The Shakers took her in and kept her alive for six more years. But after all those years of fighting her illness, she had lapsed into unbearable pain. The week before she died, she had been taken with a chill and diarrhea, which everybody knows is the last stage of consumption."

"As soon as the people in the surrounding community found out that Brother Charles was in jail, there was an uproar like you never heard. They went to the county commission and demanded that he at least be given bail, so the county commission went on record as favoring the release of Charles on a nominal bond or even on his own word. But they could not release a man who had confessed to murder. Still the crowds grew stronger every day, demanding to have him released. Finally they agreed to convene the grand jury for Wednesday of last week."

"Mr. Charles calmly told his story on Wednesday. He said, 'Sister Sadie had always told us to let her die in peace and without pain. After she asked Sister Elizabeth to let her get out of the body, she refused to eat anything at all. On Sunday night she suffered terribly and towards morning, she begged us to kill her. I went to St. Cloud at daylight and got some opiates to ease her. I gave her some on a cloth and she went to sleep. But she kept waking up. Every time I gave her more, I asked her, 'Sadie, do you want this?' And she said yes. She was suffering and didn't want to live. Finally, after the sixth time I gave her the chloroform, she went to sleep and didn't wake up. Losing Sadie has left a deep wound in my heart. I loved her as much as a father loves a child. But I answered the cry of an innocent child. I would be a monster if I hadn't.'"

"It did not take the grand jury long to reach a verdict. They refused to indict any of the Shakers, including Brother Charles!"

Ben continued, "Even though I don't think these people meant to do wrong, the law was broken. And I wonder how many more mercy killings this will lead to."

After Ben finished his story, Margaret, Catherine, and Cole discussed their own feelings about the case and then drifted into talking about ethics and religion in general. Catherine was feeling melancholy, which was not like her at all. She would miss these conversations with Margaret. Not even in Boston did she have the opportunity to participate in such rich debate about serious life issues. Cole was open to her ideas but he, like Sam, didn't relish arguing with her like Margaret did. And of course, she would miss Cole terribly, but she did not allow herself to think beyond tomorrow.

After his long storytelling, when the hot debate ensued, Ben was strangely quiet. He looked at Margaret and was reminded of a time when she had been so desperate in her mind for so many weeks that she begged him to put her out of her misery. She had even found the gun he had hidden in his office and had put it in the nightstand beside their bed. Loving Margaret as he did, Ben was racked with pain and guilt, but he was never, at any time, tempted to quiet her suffering in that way. Then, a few weeks later, as quickly as it arrived, the terrible fog inside Margaret lifted and she was happy once more.

After that, Ben had lain awake many nights, trying to identify and destroy Margaret's demons. Even though he had been unsuccessful at easing her pain, he was sure he would never be able to end her life or be a proponent of mercy killing.

After dinner the two men went to the library off the large salon and smoked cigars. Cole, as usual, said very little, but as they were getting ready to rejoin the family, he said to Ben, "Everything she told you was true, you know."

Ben said, "I'm a pretty good judge of character and I figured it was, but thanks for telling me."

Leaving the Elliotts was a bittersweet time, especially for Catherine.

The next morning, she gathered up her belongings in the hotel room. There wasn't much. She had the clothes that had been purchased since leaving the abbey and the small trunk that she had rescued from her house and then again from the barn at the Wilson's ranch. The hotel bellman put her bags on the trolley, and they drove the short distance to the train station.

After Cole had left her bed early that morning and they said goodbye, she was sure she wouldn't see him again. But as the train pulled out of the station, there he was—a short distance away, sitting on his horse. When she boarded the train, he tipped his hat and rode off in another direction.

THE GIFT OF A LIFETIME
• • •

Cole rode out past Oconee toward Sanford. The last five years had been good for him. Orange County Sheriff John Caesar Anderson had hired him as a deputy in the northern part of the county. He was able to roam the country he loved.

He hated wearing the gun, which he had drawn only twice. The first time, he shot an alligator after it had eaten a small dog at a fourth of July picnic at Lake Orienta. The second time was just a few months earlier, when, to the dismay of the entire population, a terrible freeze had come to Central Florida. Citrus crops were devastated. The frustration of the growers combined with the constant, ongoing quarrels with ranchers caused the drinking and fighting in town on Saturday nights to reach an all-time high. One particular night there was such a brawl at the Lakeside Saloon that he was forced to draw the gun and shoot it toward the ceiling, just to get everybody's attention.

Two years after Catherine went back to Boston, Cole married Josh Ulmer's daughter, Emma, and they had two baby boys within two years. Emma was a quiet, simple woman who had loved Cole most of her life. She had been raised on a fern farm in the Northeast corner of Orange County, which previously had been called Mosquito County—and for good reason.

Her father had settled in the area called Chuluota in the years just after the Civil War, when squatters could build a farm just about anywhere they wanted and sell off the cypress and pines to timber companies. At first, Josh Ulmer had hunted, trapped, and grown vegetables, but when the rich tourists began to arrive, one of them convinced him of something that he'd never known was possible. Growing ferns could be a lucrative business. After Emma had completed the 10th grade at the little schoolhouse in Chuluota, she had gone home to help her mother with the kind of work that turned young girls into old women very quickly.

The Ulmers were Methodists and, when Emma was a child, she remembered the Methodist circuit rider coming to their church once every three months to preach and conduct the business of the church. The other Sundays, Josh, who was the Sunday school superintendent, would lead the class discussions in the little wooden church on Belville Street. Cole would come to visit Emma's church on rare occasions during his time as a temporary minister, and she had fallen mightily in love the first time she laid eyes on him. She was 14 years old. She begged her mother to invite him home for Sunday dinner. They had fried chicken with cabbage and corn on the cob and little iced cakes. It was her mother's birthday and to her surprise, Emma's father presented his wife with a new crochet hook and four balls of yarn. This brought tears to her mother's eyes. Emma looked across the table at Cole with her own big moon eyes, hoping he would be inspired by her father's romantic gesture, but he was not. Many years later, after they were married, Emma tried to remind Cole of that first day they met but he remembered none of it. Not even the chicken and cabbage. Emma had waited many years for Cole to notice her, but as far as she was concerned, it had all been worth it.

Cole left his horse at the livery in Sanford and boarded the ferry to cross Lake Monroe. Others in the flat bed ferry had horses and even buggies with them. On the north side of the lake, the ferry tender tied up the pier in front of what had once been the finest hotel in Central Florida, the Brock House.

The Brock had catered to the rich and powerful northerners who came by boat down the intercoastal waterway and then into the St. Johns River that widened in the middle of the state to form the lake. President Cleveland had been one of the Brock's frequent winter visitors seeking warmth before the railroad was completed and northerners had transportation to reach inland spots. But still, a major part of the state was an unexplored wilderness. Thomas Jefferson had once said it would take 40 generations to tame the American frontier. And it would surely take even longer to tame Florida.

When Catherine had left, it took him months to fight his way out of the lonely fog that had surrounded him. Now, after all these years he was finally content with his life with Emma and his baby boys. He had made peace with himself and with God and he was finally able to go whole months without thinking of Catherine.

And then the telegram arrived: *Cole, please meet me at the Brock House, Enterprise, May. 17, 2:00 P.M. Catherine*

Cole wasn't happy. He had known logically from the first that they had no future. But he, of all people, knew that sometimes his emotions were beyond his control. This scared him—and rightly so. He got to the hotel lobby and told the desk clerk that Mrs. Hamilton was expecting him.

The clerk answered, "Yes, she is. Go right up to room 210."

When he knocked on the door, it was opened by a black woman dressed in the fine clothes that northerners tended to wear when first visiting Florida, before they had experienced the heat and the dust and the mosquitoes. He was ushered into the large sitting room. The woman took his hat, hung it on the rack by the door, and disappeared.

And then she was in the room. Still beautiful, but different from any of the ways he had seen her in their short life together. She was dressed in a simple shirtwaist dress, but even Cole could see it was made of fine material. She had put on weight, but it suited her. Her body had finally filled out. She no longer had the boyish look that had served her well when they were traveling together. Her hair was long and piled up on her head like it had been, when he first saw her, frantically digging her husband's grave. But this time, it was perfectly coifed and secured by a jeweled comb.

She walked quickly to Cole and before he could catch his breath, she hugged him and said, "It's so good to see you. I still think about you almost every day."

Cole was overcome with conflicting feelings. And the combination of love, hate, confusion, and anger was rendering him mute. Finally, he said, "Why did you call me here? I have a life now."

"I know you do. So do I. I had to come to Florida to research an article I'm writing."

Seeing the look on Cole's face, she laughed and said, "Don't worry. It's not about you—or me. It's only about the place, this part of the country. Thomas Edison has built a home and laboratory in Fort Myers, and he has agreed to an interview."

As she motioned for him to sit down, she continued, "But the reason I asked you here is because I promised you I would."

Cole looked bewildered and said, "What are you talking about?"

"First, I want to tell you what happened to me after I left Florida and went home to Boston. My father died and left me the house in Boston and a small inheritance. Then, a year or so later, Sam's estate was finally settled. It took a long time because there were no death records, no dates or times. The lawyers were finally able to establish that he was dead and that he left all his assets to me. Sam was the last in his family to die. He left me a very wealthy woman. Now I'm able to write all I want. And I have a publisher who appreciates what I write and understands what I'm trying to say."

Cole sat and examined his hands. Finally he said, "What does this have to do with me?"

Catherine called to the woman, who had answered the door, "Please send in Margaret."

A little girl bounced into the room holding the hand of an older black man.

Catherine said to Cole, "You met Mrs. Johnson at the door. This is Mr. Johnson. They travel with us."

The little girl let go of the man's hand and bounded over to where Cole and Catherine were sitting. She was wearing a pinafore and little ringlets of curls fell all over her head. She had started chattering the moment she'd entered the room.

"Hello, what's your name?" she asked Cole.

"Mine's Margaret Hamilton and I'm five."

Mr. and Mrs. Johnson stared at Cole.

There was no getting around the fact that the child looked like him—a fact that Cole had not missed.

He looked at the child and simply said, "My name's Cole." Looking into her eyes was like looking into a mirror.

Margaret burrowed her way between Cole and Catherine on the sofa, put her hand on Cole's knee and said, "My mommy says you're her friend and that makes you my friend. Did you know my daddy? He died. We're going to see his grave where my mommy and daddy lived when they were cowboys. Are you a cowboy?"

Then, touching his badge she asked, "Are you a policeman?"

Margaret kept chattering. Finally, Catherine told her to run and play with Mrs. Johnson and she would call her back in a few moments to say goodbye to Mr. Wills.

Cole watched as the child skipped out of the room. "What can I say, Catherine. I have nothing to give you."

Catherine responded, "You've already given me more than I could ever have dreamed of receiving in this life. I always thought my writing would be a way of leaving something behind. But now I have Margaret. With all the good fortune that's come to me, she is, without question, the best thing in my life. I never dreamed that God would entrust me with such a gift, through you. I wanted to let you know that Margaret exists, but I also wanted to thank you—for everything."

"Will she ever know?"

"No, she'll always be Margaret Hamilton."

Cole started to get up, but Catherine said, "Please wait. I want to give you something. You know that I have a lot of money. Probably more than you can imagine. But I know you would be angry if I tried to give you any of it and you would find a way to lose it before you got home."

Completely overwhelmed and wondering what was coming next, Cole sat back down on the sofa.

"Do you know what an insurance policy is?"

"Sort of."

"Well, I've taken out an insurance policy on your life. Your wife and sons are the beneficiaries. When you die they get the money. So, tell your wife to contact Ben Elliott if anything should happen to you."

"How much will they get?"

"Ten thousand dollars each."

Cole gulped. "I don't want this."

"I know you don't. So, stay alive, and it won't happen for a long time. They need you a lot more than they need the money."

They talked a few more moments but there was really nothing more to say. Margaret was invited back in to say goodbye to "Mommy's friend," but Catherine didn't let her prattle on as she had before.

When he was at the door, he stood with his hat in his hands and said, "So long, Catherine."

She put her arms around him. As they embraced, Catherine said, "Thank you, Cole, for saving my life." But as she held him, she was thinking about an evening when she and Margaret Elliott were reading aloud from Lord Byron's *Don Juan, VI* and Margaret read the words. *"There is a tide in the affairs of women, which, taken at the flood, leads–God knows where."*

MEET THE AUTHOR
• • •

I was born in Indianapolis, Indiana. My mother died when I was very young, so my little brother and I were sometimes farmed out to relatives, but we mostly took care of each other.

I have four children, ten grandchildren and two great grandchildren, all with deep roots in the state of Florida.

I've been a ferocious reader all my life. When I was a child, I was introduced to, and fell in love with, a book series called, "The Bears of Blue River", about pioneer days in Indiana.

My first marriage, to Ken Crossman, was filled with excitement and adventure and, occasionally, danger, here in Florida. He was a United Methodist minister. I was a consultant, platform speaker and writer. We were both caught up in the Civil Rights movement.

A year or so after Ken died, I met and later married, David Runyan. We had adventures of another kind. We traveled extensively in Europe, visiting 19 countries, and we both loved delving into the history of each place we visited.

David was born in Kulala, Lumpur, the son of Methodist missionaries. So, his life was full of adventure from the beginning.

– Cecily Crossman

CONTACT THE AUTHOR
• • •

You are welcome to connect with the author with comments about this book.

Email:

cesscrossman@hotmail.com

Connect with her on Facebook at:

Cess Crossman

Linkedin.com

Cecily Crossman

Blog:

My Best Time
cecilycrossman.com

MORE FROM THE AUTHOR
• • •

New Day
ISBN: 978-1735309101 | 78 pages
Published by Dominionhouse Publishing & Design, LLC

***

The 1960s and '70s were, in many ways, a turbulent, frustrating time of unrest. But they led to a formative time for minorities and women. These decades helped define me personally as well.

All along the way I wrote poetry as a release for my personal feelings of unrest. In 1978 I self published a slim book of poetry titled *New Day*. This was no small task prior to the Internet.

I was leading workshops and presentations for various groups at the time and began taking a few books along with me. I had no idea what to expect but we soon went through three printings. A handful of counselors used them in group therapy for those experiencing similar frustrations.

And now, 50 plus years later, I've been encouraged to republish *New Day*. I've added a few more poems that represent, for me, those life changing decades.

–Cecily Crossman

The book is available on:

**Amazon.com | BarnesandNobles.com
and where books are sold online**

More From the Author
• • •

In 2007, I started a new chapter in my life, one that would lead me all over the world with a man I adored. And, as a result, I began writing a blog, titled *My Best Time.*

What is a blog? It's simply an online diary. It can be written for your eyes only, or for specific groups of people, or for the whole world to see.

I chose the whole world.

What is my blog about? I like to say it's about me. But, in truth, it's about whatever I'm feeling excited about at any given time. I can't see who's reading, but I can see the statistics. From the time I started the blog, until this day, it's been viewed 262,895 times. It averages 2,000 views a month and what I particularly like is that it's viewed all over the world.

Following are a few of my viewers all-time favorites:

An' Live Off the Fat of the Land, posted January 26, 2009 during a recession.
Kurt Vonnegut in Indianapolis, posted November 1, 2018
Two Dishwashers, posted November 26, 2018
Martha Dodd, posted May 1, 2012
8lb. 6 oz. Baby Jesus, posted December 16, 2016
Hugh Hefner is a Scrapbooker, posted September 6, 2013

Here is a posting I wrote on October 20, 2021. It engendered a number of responses from people who've had similar experiences.

Grace

Yesterday I got pulled over by the cops! Well, it was just the one police officer. But it was exciting because when I noticed the whirling lights, I assumed he was trying to get around me, so I pulled over and sped up a bit. For about five seconds it was a high-speed chase.

• • •

Eventually I pulled into a parking lot, and he followed.

The officer could not have been kinder. He told me I was driving 15 miles over the speed limit and then went on to explain that the speed limit went down several blocks behind where we were on the street.

I told him I knew that because "I live right there," pointing to the brick wall in front of us. He asked for my driver's license, then disappeared back into his cruiser. When he returned, he handed back the license and told me to have a good day.

No ticket! But here's the thing. I broke the law. I was speeding. He knew that but still let me go.

As you know, my Meniere's Disease causes panic attacks from time to time. So how was I feeling throughout this process, from the whirling lights to the "Have a good day?"

I felt great. I felt grateful. After checking to see if I had a record, the office congratulated me for my pristine driving history. At that point I did have to confess that I had received a speeding ticket in the past – precisely – in 1972.

Since I was speeding yesterday, I totally broke the law, but, by the grace of this young, kind African American police officer, I was not charged.

The only thing that could have riled me up would have been if he let me go because I was just a little old lady driving a Camry. In that case I would have had to demand that I get the ticket and things would have gotten all weird.

But I wasn't getting that vibe. He gave me grace.

***

View my blog at cecilycrossman.com